Gus and

'This story is just all sorts of ~~...~~ enjoyed it so much. What a beautifully-put-together middle-grade novel. I mean, who couldn't love a story that features ghosts, psychics, comets, cane fields, caravans, and a dilapidated drive-in movie theatre! Victoria has done such a great job of bringing this tale to life. In fact, it was so vivid I'm sure it should (and probably will) become a movie itself. And if it does, I really would love to go and see it at a drive-in just like the Starlight! Gus is a wonderful hero and I was cheering for her and the Ables the whole way. This has the perfect mix of feels, humour and pathos, and a sprinkle of supernatural!'

— Karen Foxlee, award-winning author of
Lenny's Book of Everything and *Dragon Skin*

'A magical middle-grade book with a feather-light fantastical touch that wonderfully helps the young protagonist figure out their complex and confusing family; the hope they have in their heart for a fresh start, and the ways that the past can haunt and help us. Just – stunning!'

— Danielle Binks, award-winning author of
The Year the Maps Changed

'An utterly captivating tale of family, friends and a haunted drive-in cinema, told with gentle humour and poignant moments that tug on the heart-strings.'

— Kate Forsyth, best-selling and award-winning author of The Chain of Charms series

'A novel that is as full of heart as it is ghosts. I found myself pulled into the story of Gus and the Able family head-first. Charming, exciting, poignant. An enchanting debut.'

— Rebecca McRitchie, award-winning author of the Whimsy & Woe and Jinxed! series

'A delightfully offbeat ghost story, featuring cinema, snacks, school projects and the joy of second chances.'

— Jaclyn Moriarty, award-winning author of *The Extremely Inconvenient Adventures of Bronte Mettlestone*

'A moving and haunting read. Gus triumphs in finding her own story. This magical and quintessentially Australian tale is all about storytelling and how we have the capacity to rewrite our own destinies.'

— Yvette Poshoglian, best-selling author of the Ella and Olivia series

'A lovely, quirky, heart-warming story, about ghosts and movies and finding a home.'

— Judith Rossell, award-winning author of
Withering-by-Sea

'Quirky, sweetly nostalgic and deeply immersive. A book that quickly became a treasured friend.'

— Jen Storer, award-winning author of
the Truly Tan series

Gus AND THE Starlight

VICTORIA CARLESS

Angus&Robertson
An imprint of HarperCollins*Children'sBooks*

Angus&Robertson

An imprint of HarperCollins*Children'sBooks*, Australia

HarperCollins*Publishers*
Australia • Brazil • Canada • France • Germany • Holland • Hungary
India • Italy • Japan • Mexico • New Zealand • Poland • Spain • Sweden
Switzerland • United Kingdom • United States of America

First published in Australia in 2022
by HarperCollins*Publishers* Australia Pty Limited
ABN 36 009 913 517
harpercollins.com.au

Copyright © Victoria Carless 2022

The right of Victoria Carless to be identified as the author of this work
has been asserted by her in accordance with the *Copyright Amendment
(Moral Rights) Act 2000*.

This work is copyright. Apart from any use as permitted under the *Copyright
Act 1968*, no part may be reproduced, copied, scanned, stored in a retrieval
system, recorded, or transmitted, in any form or by any means, without the
prior written permission of the publisher.

A catalogue record for this book is available
from the National Library of Australia

ISBN 978 1 4607 6064 2 (paperback)
ISBN 978 1 4607 1392 1 (ebook)

Cover design by HarperCollins Design Studio
Cover illustration © Jessica Cruickshank
Author photograph by Katie Bennett
Typeset in Sabon LT Std by Kelli Lonergan
Printed and bound in Australia by McPherson's Printing Group

MIX
Paper from
responsible sources
FSC
www.fsc.org   FSC® C001695

For Minnie

Chapter 1

The screen door burst open, slapping against the faded weatherboards. Gus jumped in the middle seat where she waited with her brother and sister in the sky-blue sedan.

Through the grimy windscreen she saw her mother wrestling their beat-up suitcase down the front path, the hem of her cheesecloth dress snagging on dandelions. The flowers looked nice, but they were a weed, Gus knew, and nobody cared for them.

Mrs Able wore jeans and sneakers under her dress and a brown cardigan over it, as well as the tartan coat that had once been Gran's. Gus and her siblings wore most of their clothes too, including pyjamas under their school uniforms and their shabby winter coats, all bought from Salvos.

The Camry was whining, the engine nagging at their mother to hurry up. Beside her, Alice, Gus's big sister by one year, leaned her head against the window, her breath fogging up the glass. Her posture was resigned. Her whole body said, *Here we go again*.

Their little brother, Artie, was kicking the driver's seat and wailing he'd left his Transformers inside. Gus knew she should go get them, but her stomach hurt and her feet were tingly and she was having trouble breathing. She worried if she moved she would shatter into tiny pieces, so she stayed put, immobile in the middle seat, hoping she wouldn't spontaneously combust.

She felt the boot fling open and heard her mother toss the heavy suitcase in. Inside the case everything would be jumbled, all the possessions they owned which had followed them from house to house, cracked and nearly broken things, worn down and out by wear.

Then Mrs Able was in the driver's seat, throwing her handbag beside her. She said something low and swear-y as she flung the gearstick into reverse. The children in the backseat collectively released the breath they'd been holding and the family slid backwards down the driveway. Putting the car into gear, their mother angled the Camry down the street and, just like that, they were gone.

Gus watched their suburb, home for the last few months, flash by. Here the houses all looked the same, gappy timber workers' cottages that hunkered against the southerlies, their paint tired and their furniture mismatched. They were places full of things the owners hadn't chosen for themselves. They were houses where no one stayed long enough to give them any love.

As her mother drove Troy's car away from the place that had Troy's name on the lease, Gus looked out the window and saw they had reached the high street, with its graffitied tram stops, the stores that sold fake flowers and the chicken takeaway shops and their smell of hot chips and grease. Gus felt light-headed and didn't know if it was because she was hungry, or because of what had happened earlier that evening. She saw their dinner — frozen meals from a box, mushy and steaming from the microwave — going soggy at the table.

She concentrated on making a list, the way Gran had shown her. Gus began to list books she had read.

It didn't matter what she listed, Gran had told her. It could be books, or the periodic table of elements, the names of the pet fish who had swum briefly in and out of their lives, or the list of streets on which they had lived. The important thing was making an inventory in her head to distract herself.

Gus got to *Little Women* before she became aware of the car again, and the warmth generated by the crush of the three siblings in the backseat. Their mother nudged the accelerator further to the floor and they sped towards the highway exit.

At Gus's feet was the library book she had borrowed the week before, *Matilda*, a story she had read so many times it felt like they were old friends. Also at her feet were the sandwiches in a paper bag that Alice had smashed together on their way out the door, an unappetising mix of stale bread and jam for their dinner. It was going to be a meals on wheels night — with a difference — again. In fact, by the look of their mother's determined driving, they might be on the road for some time.

As they approached the library, which was on the last turn-off before the highway, Gus retrieved the book at her feet and held it aloft.

'Mum?' she said. 'Can I just—?'

Their mother glanced back at her sharply. The look on her face made Gus halt.

'We're not stopping tonight,' her mother said.

Gus opened her mouth to protest. Not returning the book was like stealing. She would get a fine, the late fees a blemish on her otherwise perfect library record. She'd been hoping to get a library card of her own soon. She'd only ever had temporary ones, on account of them not having a permanent address.

Alice gave Gus a look, one that said, Don't even start.

They definitely weren't stopping tonight. It was lucky she hadn't made any friends here, Gus thought, as she wouldn't have been able to say goodbye.

Their mother's phone lit up on the front passenger seat and the jangly ring tone cut through the silence in the car. They ignored it but Gus saw Mrs Able tighten her grip on the steering wheel.

It is so lucky, she repeated to herself, that I don't have anyone to miss. That had been something she had learned, a special trick cultivated along the way. Gus was really good now at not making any friends at all.

The mobile screeched again and Gus's stomach contracted. This time, Mrs Able glanced over at it. Her face told them who the caller was. Troy would be wondering where they were. He would be wondering about the payment he'd decided he was due. The deal had been they could only stay in his house if their mother did psychic readings for cash.

'Can't we say goodbye to Troy?' Artie whined.

He was the youngest, so he was still learning about their mother's looks, the secret code Alice and Gus had begun to understand as they grew. The looks that said, *Don't ask, girls*. Or the one that said, *I'm OK, kids*, when she clearly wasn't.

Artie was still learning about what their mother did for a living, why she was visited at odd hours by strangers asking questions about their dead relatives. Why she sat at a folding table in a corner of the lounge room with these strangers, lighting candles and speaking in hushed tones. And why, sometimes, she or they cried.

Artie was especially still learning how people like Troy, who 'managed their mother's affairs', and were their sometimes-fathers, often took the bigger cut.

Troy would probably be at the pub now, Gus knew. He'd be trying to make some money on the dogs with his tracksuit-wearing associates. Or worse, he'd be trying to rustle up more business. Troy had been short of money lately, some deal gone bad, and had got angry when the couple who had sat at the card table in their house that evening had refused to pay. Their mother hadn't been able to reach their son's spirit. In Troy's view, this was entirely her fault, both that she'd failed to contact the dead man and because she didn't get the money upfront.

But Gus knew that sometimes this happened and her mother wasn't actually to blame. She had noticed that sometimes ghosts just didn't want to be found by the living. Being at the table with dark-clothed strangers, trying to call up their lost loved ones, was her mother's job, but it didn't seem to be her choice. And it wasn't a job she could forget about out of work hours either.

Gus recalled how after most readings lately their mother disappeared to her bedroom, pale and drained. She would emerge the next morning, her forehead ridged with worries and her blue-grey eyes flicking around the room, chasing spectres. Gus knew her mother wanted to help the people who came to their door, desperate for contact with their dead, but her so-called gift was taking its toll.

Tonight, after the black-clad woman and man had left, and before he had gone to the pub, Troy had ranted and thrown their mother's belongings around the room.

Their mother had taken this latest frenzy, the worst one yet, as their cue to leave, bundling the children up like charity shop wares as soon as Troy left the house.

Gus wondered what Troy would do when he found out they had taken his car.

Their mother's mobile screeched again. It was Troy's name flashing on the screen.

'Block him, would you, please?' their mother asked Alice via the rear-view mirror.

Alice nodded and reached around Gus to take the phone from the front seat. She did as their mother asked and then tossed the mobile on the floor, shoving it out of sight with her foot.

'Muh-um,' Artie whined.

'We're not stopping,' their mother said again.

It was almost like she was telling herself as much as them.

'Awwwww,' Artie said.

Now Alice shot their brother her *Don't* look. Gus, on a reflex, tickled Artie, who couldn't help but laugh and squirm away from her.

He quietened down after that and the three of them sat still as stones in the backseat.

As Mrs Able looked at the children in the rear-view mirror, Gus saw her mother's mouth was pressed into a line.

Gus gazed out the window at the city rushing by. 'Goodbye house, goodbye street, goodbye school, goodbye library, goodbye trams, goodbye chicken shops,' she said under her breath. Gus said goodbye the way she had to plenty of other places, plenty of times before.

She looked up at the night sky, which was an inky velvet now, with the first star of evening peeping through.

'Goodbye, Troy,' she added.

This one she said out loud, willing it to be final.

Chapter 2

They slept draped over each other in the backseat like a pile of puppies while their mother drove through the night.

Gus half-woke a few times, such as when they passed through a cluster of streetlights watching over a sleeping town. Other times it was when a semi-trailer overtook them, the rumble of the truck's tyres and the throaty roar of the engine a kind of late-night lullaby.

One time when Gus woke, Mrs Able had the demister and the wipers on, accompaniments to the hum of midnight wind. And always the headlights, casting a low-down moonlight over the slate road with its mesmerising dotted line.

Driving in the dark on the empty highway was like being in space, Gus thought. She felt weightless, their tinny car bobbing in the universe, like a strange astronomical body, a lost star maybe.

Another time when she opened her eyes, Gus thought for a moment she was under the sea, the deepest darkest part where the strange fish dwelled, those glimpsed in the furthest underwater room in the aquarium, the one hardly anyone visited.

Only once during the night did Gus wake properly. Her mother stopped for petrol, and the lights of the service station glimmered through the windscreen like those of an alien ship. She blinked and rubbed her eyes, momentarily afraid her family would be beamed up. She was relieved when she saw her mother through the servo window, the glass thick with condensation, buying supplies. Gus's belly gnawed at her. The jam sandwiches were long gone and so when her mother handed her a bottle of strawberry milk as she slipped back into the driver's seat Gus was grateful.

'Share it with the others,' her mother said.

But she smiled as she said it and Gus knew it was their little secret. Sometimes she pretended she was her mother's favourite. She had to be someone's favourite, didn't she? It was a law of the universe, she felt sure. She just hadn't figured out whose yet. There was still time, however. She was only nearly-twelve, after all. It was going to be her birthday in a month. Perhaps she would know more then; about how not to make friends or avoid imploding from worry. About how not to become like her mother.

Gus regarded her siblings from the middle seat. Artie, now dressed in his dinosaur pyjamas, was snoring lightly, his sandy hair all mussed. His mouth was open, revealing his five missing teeth. He was like that, Artie, a kid who did everything at once, including losing all his front teeth. He would miss his mates in Year One. He had fared the best of them with the spin-cycle of house moves they had been through.

Alice still looked pretty, even as she slept upright in the car. Her honey-coloured hair shimmered around her pale face and her mouth rested in a perfect bow. She even sleeps neatly, Gus thought.

In contrast, Gus's mousy-brown hair, usually cut in a bob, stuck up all over. She could feel a crust of drool that had formed by her lip.

People often couldn't believe she and Alice were sisters. It was true the children had different fathers. Even so, they shared a firecracker of a mother and that was surely the bigger portion of their makeup and the thing that bound them? Still, the sisters were like chalk and cheese, their mother always said. Gus wondered which one she was supposed to be.

Gus was surprised that Alice and Artie had been able to sleep at all. They had been on the road together before, but not like this. They hadn't ever driven through the night. Instead, they had shuffled through the suburbs of the city, in and out of borrowed houses, borrowed cars, borrowed lives. Troy's was the tenth house Gus could recall, but she thought there were maybe others too, from before she could remember.

Her favourite place had been Gran's house, where they had stayed before Mum met Troy. The months in the tin-roofed fibro shack on the farm by the sea, while their mother picked fruit nearby, had been heaven. They had all become tanned and wild that summer, even Alice, who had worn her bathers at the table and squirted sauce with abandon on the sausages Gran had cooked up.

The best thing about Gran's place was that it was on a back road. There hadn't been any late-night knocks on the door then.

Instead of visitors seeking spiritual contact, Gran had souvenir tablecloths and a ginger cat called Timothy, as well as extra tins of food and packets of lollies in the pantry ('in case of the apocalypse, darling'). She handed out thawed homemade lamingtons at afternoon tea (still a bit frozen in the middle) and read them books she had dug up, books that had once been their mother's, even when Gus and Alice were really too old to be read to.

Gus had pored over these books after lights out with Gran's Dolphin torch, turning the yellowed pages, marvelling that her mother's hands had turned them also when she was Gus's age. These were the books that had helped her mother get a scholarship at university in the city, where she had met Alice's father and before it had all gone bad. Before her abilities were uncovered, first by friends at parties and later by boyfriends, who urged her to charge for spiritual readings. After Alice, Gus and Artie arrived, she was sometimes forced to use her gifts to afford food and rent. Troy, who Mum had first met when fruit-picking on a farm neighbouring Gran's, had been the most recent example of this. Troy had also been the one to convince them to move back to the city with him.

As her mother flicked the indicator to turn out of the servo and get back on the highway, a young woman appeared in front of their car.

14

The woman wore an old-fashioned white dress, and her red hair was wild, escaping from two long plaits. She looked very pale, as though coated in road dust. She seemed lost.

Gus's heart stilled. Time had stopped and she was stuck in this moment like a moth caught in the bath.

The woman stared at her mother through the windscreen and Gus knew what the woman was saying, though nobody said a word. The woman's eyes said, *Help me.*

Gus's mother exhaled shakily and, instead of stopping the car, put the Camry in reverse. They drove backwards, away from the pale woman, over the length of the service station until the white figure was tiny like a toy, a bug, a speck, until she was invisible and Gus wondered if she had really been there at all.

But she knew. Gus knew the woman both had and hadn't been there, because she could only be a ghost, couldn't she? Did that mean …?

Shaking, Gus looked into the rear-view mirror and saw blue-grey eyes, so like her own, as her mother pulled out of the servo and back onto the highway.

'Go back to sleep,' her mother whispered. 'We've a way to go yet.'

Gus couldn't reply. She knew she mustn't tell anyone, especially not her mother, about what she had just seen. That would make it true.

Instead, Gus leaned her head back against the seat. They seemed to be heading north. It was a feeling rather than any road sign that told her this.

Gus watched her mother sip from the plastic bottle of spring water she had bought, before closing her eyes again. Her mother didn't believe in buying bottled water so that's when Gus knew for sure they weren't going back.

Chapter 3

They drove for four days up the east coast and most of it through rain. They played I Spy, car bingo and the licence plate game. They played guess-the-TV-show-theme-song and count-the-cow/sheep/blades of grass. They made up stories about the fantastical lives of people they saw at rest stops and bickered until even they were sick of it. They ate junk food until they were bouncing off the seats and then passed out from the sugar highs.

While her brother and sister dozed, Gus made lists in her head. One was titled *Names I'd Prefer to be Called*. On that list she included: Abigail, Clara, Gabriella, Kirsten, Kristen, Jodie, Iona, Maddie, Penelope, Riley, Sasha and Willow — practically anything other than Augusta.

Another list was called *Characters I'd Like to be Friends With.*

A further list that popped into her head before she could shut it out was *Things I Wish Mum Hadn't Seen.* She crumpled that list in her mind quick-smart.

What they didn't do to pass the time was talk about Troy, or the missed calls from him. Even though they'd blocked his number, she knew Troy wouldn't give up easily. They had all been relieved when their mother stopped at the post office in one nondescript town to buy a new sim card and organise a new number for her phone so he couldn't reach or track them.

They also didn't talk about the dissatisfied couple in black clothes, or the fact they drove Troy's car, or the rent money their mum apparently owed him. They didn't mention the set of their mother's mouth either.

At dusk each night Mrs Able pulled into public campgrounds, which were mostly empty. They used the shower blocks that universally rained cold water and brushed their teeth at the tin sinks under snapping fluorescent lights. They slapped at bugs before piling back into the sky-blue Camry, their smells now infused in the seats. Their mother laid the backseat down so the kids could stretch out to sleep. They nestled together there like a tray of spoons, while their mother slept practically upright like a horse in the driver's seat.

It reminded Gus of when she and Alice had slept together in the same bed in a warm bright room under a dusty striped blanket. Which house and which suburb and which sometimes-father had that been? She hadn't minded being so close to Alice then, and she wondered if Alice remembered that now, too. They had been each other's shadows for so long, since they were tiny girls. Together they built forts and played games only the two of them knew the rules for: Alien Inventors and Doggy Daycare and Fairy Unicorn Princesses Under the Sea. Alice had taught Gus everything: how to read, how to code, as well as how to get a thin smear of jam right to the crust of her bread. Now Alice barely said anything to Gus, or to anybody.

Gus missed sharing everything with Alice. When they had stayed with Gran on the farm by the beach, on those summer nights it had stormed, Gus had pretended to be afraid and climbed into the big bed with Gran. She felt safe there while the sky rattled and raged, breaking open again and again.

Every morning at the public campgrounds they rose groggily, sleep still gumming their eyes as they stepped over the dewy grass to wash their faces and drink from the shower-block tap. They scoffed the bananas and muesli bars their mother handed out and then climbed back into the car for another day's drive. Their mother didn't say where they were going, or even when they might get there. She especially didn't say what they would do when they arrived, and this was also different from the other times they had taken off, in a hurry to someplace new.

Usually their mother had an exit plan for when things went bad after a reading, or with one of the sometimes-fathers: they'd crash at a friend's, or find a cheap motel. There were always customers in her line of business. Their mother could set up a stall at the local markets or advertise online. Gus had fervently hoped they were going to Gran's again but after the second day of driving they had sailed past the exit to her small town. Gran's house was a silent but definite no.

Still Gus, Alice and Artie didn't dare ask questions, as long as Mrs Able's mouth stayed in that line. Perhaps Mrs Able didn't even know where they were heading herself.

Gus had been right though, they were travelling north. She could tell because day by day it got warmer, even though it was autumn. They'd had to peel off layers of clothes until they were down to shorts and T-shirts. Their pale legs fed gleeful mosquitos at dusk.

When they reached the northern state on the third day of driving, they were all ready to disown each other. The rain hadn't let up and the children were exhausted from arguing and inflicting arm burns at close range. Their mother's lips had all but disappeared and her severe expression looked set to become permanent.

For another day or so they seemed to pass through a new town or hamlet every hour or so, each containing a drycleaner, a takeout shop and a centenary park with one and a half swings. Sometimes they stopped for petrol, or cold drinks, or at roadside stands to buy bags of tropical fruit with ants and bugs still on them. So when their mother braked abruptly late one afternoon in the main street of a town much like any other, Gus didn't really think much of it.

After they'd jerked to a stop, Mrs Able got out of the car. 'Wait here, you lot,' she instructed.

Then she pulled her brown cardigan over her head and stepped out into the rain.

It was sheeting down by then and Gus could barely make out her mother's form as she disappeared into the golden haze of a fish and chip shop. The sign said *Calvary Takeaway*.

Their mother placed her order at the counter with a teenage girl in a hairnet and began to peruse a community noticeboard while she waited. Mrs Able took a slip of paper from the board and pocketed it. She went up to the counter again and said something to the bored-looking cashier.

Gus wondered what the paper said. She guessed they weren't getting a pet kitten any time soon. Alice's nose was pressed to the glass, and Gus peered past her sister's shoulder through the rain. Now her mother was talking to a middle-aged man in a flannel shirt and apron, presumably the takeaway shop owner and head chef. The girl wandered off to the back of the shop and removed their order from the fryer.

'What's Mum up to?' Gus wondered aloud.

The fish and chip shop man called someone on the phone while their mother waited at the counter. There was a short exchange, during which the shop owner appeared to be indicating to her mother they return in the direction from which they came. Gus's stomach dipped.

The girl in the hairnet reappeared and handed over their order, bundled in white paper. Their mother thanked the girl and the fish and chip shop owner. They nodded and went back to helm the deep fryer.

Mrs Able raced through the deluge back to their car and opened the door, bringing a tropical downpour with her. 'Share them round,' she said, handing the now-sodden package of chips over to the children in the back seat. 'That's dinner.'

They dived on the food like seagulls, while their mother sat in the front seat, watching them. The pressed line of her mouth had upturned into a cautious smile.

Gus barely had time to register this miracle when another car pulled up alongside them, a shiny maroon sedan. The driver's side window rolled down and a woman maybe in her early fifties with her hair in curlers was revealed. Her red nails rested on the steering wheel as she idled beside the Camry. Her red lips were lined in a colour different from her lipstick. She looked like an out-of-work movie star.

The woman regarded them for a moment. When she spoke, her voice was tinkly. 'I presume you are *Delphine*? Who enquired about the job and *lodgings*?'

'Yes,' replied their mother. 'I am Delphine Able. And these are my children: Alice, Augusta and Arthur.'

'I'm *Deirdre*,' the woman said. 'Miss Deirdre *Cronk*.'

She extended her fingers in greeting, but did not quite touch their mother's hand, as though not wanting to get dirty. She regarded the children in the backseat, sitting among all their worldly possessions, eating takeaway in their second-hand clothes. Was she looking down her nose at them? Gus wondered. Or maybe that was just the woman's face. Deirdre Cronk's nose was set at a very specific angle. It didn't help that Artie had inserted a chip in each nostril.

Deirdre didn't indicate whether they had passed muster. Instead, she touched her foot to the accelerator and the maroon car lurched a little.

'Follow *me*, Delphine,' said the woman. '*I'll* lead the way.'

Chapter 4

They drove away from the takeaway place in the main street, past the park with one and a half swings. This town also had a small squat library building with its doors closed against the rain, and the Ables, Gus noted. They were indeed heading back the way they had come.

They followed the maroon sedan back onto the highway until Gus worried the woman was actually leading them out of town like unwanted interlopers, as though they had already failed some local test, one unknown to their family. Gus wondered what her mother had signed them up for. What job could possibly exist in this nondescript town for Mrs Able? Dinner felt leaden in her tummy.

Deirdre turned left down an unnamed road bordered by tall crops of sugarcane. Her mother followed obediently in the Camry. The rain had eased, though the evening was closing in and the sky was now slate-like grey. Then Deirdre turned right and from the middle seat Gus saw what the woman intended for them.

When Gus first glimpsed the Starlight, she gasped.

The place was announced by a red and yellow sign lit up with old-fashioned-type lights. The sign read: *The Starlight Drive-In Movie Theatre*. Underneath in tiny lettering were also the words: *(and drycleaners)*.

Her brother and sister had a similar reaction.

Artie, taking the chips from his nose finally, said, 'Wowee!'

Alice, speechless, pressed her pretty nose to the window, squashing it snout-like against the glass.

As their car crept up the Starlight driveway, which was edged in painted white stones, the overhead lights came on, bright as those in a sports stadium. Ahead, Gus saw a towering white movie screen, looming over a threadbare-grassed field with concrete parking spots spaced a metre or so apart. There were also white posts with radio-like boxes dotted all over the place. Gus wondered what they were for. Thick gnarled trees were clumped along the property fence line.

'Mango trees,' her mother remarked. 'We can have fruit salad next summer.'

Gus and Artie exchanged a glance. They had rarely stopped anywhere for more than a season, and it was only May.

The maroon car braked in front, beside a two-storey cement block building, so they stopped too. The siblings looked at each other, mystified, in the backseat.

Deirdre Cronk got out first. Gus saw she was wearing a quilted dressing gown, emerald-green in colour, and glittery lounge slippers. Fascinated, the children and Mrs Able tumbled out of their car too.

Noticing their stares Deirdre said, 'Oh, don't mind me and my *glad-rags*.' She giggled girlishly. 'Friday is the day I set my *hair*, while making my slimming carrot *soup*.'

The children stared some more. Deirdre's voice was singsong-y, like the classroom canary's at Gus's last school, even when the boys taught it to swear. She had a particular way of emphasising certain words.

'Oh no, Miss Cronk,' said their mother, 'not at all. Most Friday afternoons, you'll find me doing exactly the same thing.'

The children gaped at their mother's posh voice and bald-faced lie. Even Deirdre looked doubtful as she glanced at their mother's dress/jeans/Ugg boot ensemble.

'Well anyway, *welcome* to the Starlight Drive-In Movie Theatre (and drycleaners),' Deirdre said, gesturing grandly at the field of weeds and muddy puddles. 'Our family business since *1956*. Come *on*, children, and I'll give you an exclusive *tour*.'

Speechless, the Able family followed Deirdre through the puddles to the building, which had an awning out front. The first floor was mostly open at the sides and set out with mismatched tables and chairs. A kitchen area lurked at the back, as well as a drinks fridge and stainless-steel counter with a cash register and a stand of snack foods.

'This is The Moonbeam Cafe,' Deirdre explained. 'Until *recently*, the kitchen was *my* domain. We serve *hot* food to our theatre patrons. Fish burgers, savoury mince, pineapple fritters, *that* sort of thing. Crowd pleasers, *you know*. I've *tried* to expand the palates of the *locals* in recent years: beef *stroganoff*, quiche *Lorraine*, cabbage *dim sum*. All an acquired taste, *apparently*. But I draw the *line* at BYO. Outside takeaways are *strictly* not allowed. I can't *abide* wrappers strewn everywhere.'

She regarded them to see if they were keeping up.

'Don't look so *worried*, Delphine,' she tinkled. 'My recipes *will* be provided to ensure *quality* control. Despite their *limited palates*, our customers have *high expectations*, you see. My strawberry milkshakes are *famous*, I don't skimp on the *syrup*, dear. You *can* cook, I assume, Mrs Able?'

Deirdre said that last bit to their mother as an afterthought.

Gus gulped. She thought of the fish fingers they often had for dinner, still frozen in the middle, which she, Alice and Artie slathered in sauce to help them go down. She recalled the burned toast they ate at least a few times a week, especially when money was tight. How could her mother possibly run the Moonbeam Cafe?

Yet their mother nodded confidently, as though there was no reason anyone should doubt her abilities in the kitchen. 'Oh yes, I love to cook,' Mrs Able replied.

This was news to Gus. Alice, whose face was normally inscrutable, looked concerned. Artie opened his mouth to say something, but their mother squeezed his hand to indicate he stay quiet.

'*Right*, that's the Moonbeam *sorted*, then,' Deirdre said, sounding pleased. With a sweeping gesture, she indicated the field and the strange assembly of posts and radios. 'You'll also need to *regularly* inspect and maintain the outdoor *cinema* equipment,' she said.

They all followed her hand with their gaze.

'I'll *admit* the place has been *let go* a little. My father found it *difficult* to keep up with the *maintenance* in recent years. He turned *seventy-five* last *June*. *Imagine* not wanting to retire at *that* age! He's needed to hand over the *reins* for some *time* if you ask *me*.'

A cloudy look passed over her face, but she composed herself.

'I understand,' said Mrs Able.

'Suffice to *say*, my skills are needed elsewhere,' Deirdre said. 'I have given the Starlight my *all*, and yet what has it given *me*?' She looked at them, but no one was able to find an answer. 'I'll *tell* you what: unfulfilled *dreams* and dishpan *hands*, Delphine.'

'I'm, I'm sorry to hear that, Deirdre — I mean Miss Cronk,' their mother said, looking startled.

'*Anyway*, it's fortunate that *you* called. I placed that ad for a drive-in caretaker *weeks* ago at Calvary Takeaway, and I *confess* I was starting to get a little *worried*. But it appears things have worked out for the *best*. Now I'm getting *four* for the price of *one*,' she trilled.

She peered at them and Gus had the impression of mice being scrutinised by a cat.

'None of your children appear to be of the minimum working *age*, Delphine. Therefore, I will pay only *one* wage, plus twenty per cent of ticket takings, as *motivation*. I assume *cash* would be preferred, given you appear to be on, er, *benefits*. From this *wage* I will subtract *rent* on the accommodation provided. *Agreed?*'

'Uh yes, agreed,' said their mother nervously.

'*Nevertheless*, the children *will* help out, Delphine. I *myself* was an unpaid trainee in the family business for *many* years and look where it has got *me*.'

She drew herself up to her full height and the family obliged by staring at her.

'Yes, they'll, er, help out,' Mrs Able assured Deirdre.

'Good. Right, where *were* we? Ah yes, the *equipment*. I *assure* you it was a state-of-the-art *set-up* in its day,' Deirdre explained. 'My grandparents, who opened the Starlight in 1956, installed the best of *everything*. My father *followed* their lead and made some upgrades in the 1980s, when the drive-in had a *spike* in *popularity*.'

'That makes sense.' Mrs Able nodded.

'Hmmm,' said Deirdre. 'For the *audio*, patrons mostly use the speakers you see on the posts or their car radios, which should be tuned to three-ninety-six FM on the *dot* at every post, and it goes without *saying* it is a fifty-eight-foot screen. Though that doesn't seem to impress *this* community. Everyone *following*?'

They nodded, mesmerised by Deirdre Cronk.

'There are some rules to note. Patrons are to park *parallel* and no hooligans, inebriates or *people in uncovered footwear* admitted. Do you understand, Delphine?'

'Three-ninety-six FM and no uncovered footwear. Got it,' Mrs Able repeated.

Gus herself hadn't understood most of what Deirdre was saying, though she had to admit all the numbers sounded impressive.

Apparently convinced they had this in hand, Deirdre continued. '*Capacity* is three hundred and sixty cars, though we haven't had those numbers in a *long* time. People used to come from *all over* to see a double bill.'

'That's incredible,' said their mother, gazing up at the massive white screen. She had a glazed look in her eye. She was probably imagining having to make savoury mince for three hundred and sixty cars' worth of people.

'Yes, it *is* impressive,' Deirdre agreed. 'The Starlight Drive-In Movie Theatre (and drycleaners) was *unrivalled* in its day, the *jewel* of outdoor movie theatres up and down the east *coast*. I've *tried* to capitalise on my grandfather's legacy and bring a touch of *class* to the movies we screen. Sadly, my efforts screening French New Romantic Bourgeoisie cinema have *not* been supported by the general *populace*. The great *unwashed* living in *town*, with their home theatre knockoff *plasma* screens, or *whatever*, wouldn't be able to tell an *arthouse* film from their *elbows*.'

She pursed her lips in the general direction of Calvary.

'Oh, I see,' said Mrs Able.

'Perhaps you'll have *better* luck selecting movies, but I *doubt* it, with those fish-killing, meat-pie-eating *ingrates* to please,' Deirdre said, practically spitting the words down the hill towards town. She paused to straighten her dressing gown. 'My father and I sometimes disagreed about *programming*, as well,' Deirdre explained. 'Though now that he's *gone*—' She stopped herself, biting her lip theatrically. Tears welled in her eyes and she wiped them with a perfectly manicured hand.

'Gone?' repeated Mrs Able. 'As in, he's left town? Or … or something else?'

There was dread in her mother's voice. Gus was jolted out of the moment and reminded of their reality and that they were running from ghosts. The last thing her mum needed was more dead people hanging around.

'I'm, I'm not sure *exactly* what happened to him,' Deirdre said tremulously. 'One day he was *here*, counting the float for the ticket booth, and the next he was just … *gone*. *Vanished*. Poor Dad!'

She let out an anguished sob. Artie hiccupped, his eyes wide.

'Everyone's *told* me I shouldn't blame *myself*,' Deirdre added, her voice wobbly.

'Of course, and why would you?' Mrs Able replied soothingly.

'I *certainly* didn't drive him away, as the gossips in *town* think. I've given my *life* to the Starlight, sacrificed my *own* dreams of being on the *silver screen*, which I was *often* told in my girlhood was a career I'd be most suited *to*. So when I merely *suggested* we shake

34

things up a little, make some *changes* to the place — and don't think my father hasn't got money squirrelled *away*, Delphine.'

'Oh, I wouldn't think that,' their mother assured Deirdre.

'He refused *outright* to see reason. My taking over the Starlight would be the *best* course of action, I'm sure you'll agree. But when I *said* that, and suggested he sign the place over to me, you know, as *Power of Eternity*, well, he took off. Just *vanished*. And now I'm *completely* hamstrung. Suspended in *limbo*.'

'I'm sorry, Miss Cronk, I don't mean to be insensitive,' their mother said then. 'But hamstrung how? What I mean to say is—'

'It's none of your *business*? Quite *right*,' Deirdre said, her lips tight.

Their mother looked mortified. 'I'm so sorry, Miss Cronk, I didn't mean to—'

Deirdre waved her hand, indicating Mrs Able should hush. 'I'm not as bereft as I *once was*. It's been nearly *two months* since he went missing, so—'

'Excuse me, Deirdre, Miss Cronk, but can I just clarify,' Mrs Able cut in, 'is your father missing? Or, or something else? If your father has ... passed on,

I'm not sure we can ... I just — we've had our fair share of — of loss also, and — and ...'

'Oh, I understand your concern *completely*. I'm the *very* same way. It's the *river* beyond the paddocks that has *me* worried,' Deirdre confided. 'Dad used to like to toddle down there to *fish*. He had a little *hut* he built there some years ago, where he would stay when we had the odd blow-up, or should I say *artistic differences*. But it's *abandoned*, according to the authorities. There was probably a tragic *accident*, I'm told. It is a very *murky* river. The local police have investigated *extensively* but Sergeant Peters is pretty much *convinced* Dad's left us for *good*. If you get my *meaning*.'

Deirdre produced a tissue from her green dressing gown and dabbed at her eyes, delicately, like a soap actress. She raised her eyes heavenwards and sniffed, bravely.

'I like to think he's up *there*, in the great movie theatre in the *sky*, *watching down* on me,' she confided.

'Oh, Miss Cronk,' said their mother, her eyes welling up with tears too.

'Oh *Delphine*,' Deirdre Cronk said, throwing herself into their mother's arms.

She cried passionately for a time and their mother patted her back all the while. The children waited patiently for Deirdre to recover, though Artie did get distracted by some passing ants. The Able siblings were used to big displays of emotion, due to their mother's line of work. Eventually Deirdre released her grip on their mother.

'So it's *settled* then,' she said. '*You'll* be the caretakers, Delphine. My father is probably smiling down from *heaven* to see a family like *you* looking after his place.'

Deirdre sighed dramatically. The Able family looked at each other, doubtfully.

'As I was saying, I'd run the drive-in *myself*,' Deirdre continued. 'Certainly, I'm more than *qualified*. But it's *my* time to *shine*, and I *don't* mean in the kitchen. I'm afraid right now I've got a *lot* on my *plate*, what with being recently appointed the *Director* of our local Amateur Dramatic Society.'

She paused, as though waiting for them to marvel. Looking a tad disappointed when they didn't, Deirdre added, 'I've been waiting in the wings for *years* for this role. Cooking curried prawns in that kitchen, I *dreamed* of this moment. I have big plans for the dramatic society's *expansion*, starting with our *repertoire*. We're doing *Les Misérables* in June. I'm to direct *and* play Cosette. *Fortunately*, I am one of those *rare* performers who can age *up or down* for a character.'

The Able family gaped at the woman in the green velvet dressing gown.

'*Anyway*,' she said, sounding a touch disappointed by their silence, 'the Starlight is relatively *easy* to operate. We've already established who will be head *chef*,' she said.

She smiled thinly at Gus's mother.

'The next important job is *ticket collector*. This person will need to *greet* the patrons at the ticket booth by the entrance, take the *money*, give the correct *change* and direct them to their *spot*. My father left a *modest* float in the cash tin which I'll entrust *you* to manage. I *will* know however, if there is so much as a *gold coin* unaccounted for.' Deirdre paused. 'For this role, I need someone *switched on* and good at *maths*.'

She considered the row of Able children, then pointed her chin at Alice. '*You'll* have to do, I suppose.'

'Thanks,' said Alice. 'I think.'

It was more words than her sister had spoken practically the whole day.

'We'll *also* need a waiter-slash-speaker-tuner-slash-general-dogsbody. This is a *junior* position, though nonetheless *crucial* to the drive-in *operations*,' Deirdre mused.

The incoming Director of the Amateur Dramatic Society pointed one bony finger at Artie, who shrank against their mother's skirt.

'I have a sixth *sense* about casting, and on this occasion, I choose *you*,' Deirdre informed Gus's little brother.

'OK,' squeaked Artie.

'And let me *see*, what is left?' Deirdre continued. 'What am I *forgetting*?'

'Um,' ventured Gus, surprised to hear herself speak up, 'how do you get the movies on the big screen?'

'Of *course*!' Deirdre said in an affected way. 'Aren't you *clever*?' she said, tapping Gus's forehead with a red fingernail. 'To the *projection* room, everyone!'

Deirdre led the way up the cement stairs to the rooms above the cafe, with the Able family following. They reached the landing and with trepidation stood before a blue door.

Deirdre retrieved a set of keys from the pocket of her quilted robe and selected one to put in the lock.

'Are you ready to see where the *magic* happens?' she asked, her hand poised on the doorknob.

Gus had the feeling Deirdre had rehearsed this line.

'Yes,' she whispered, in lieu of anyone else speaking.

Deirdre flung open the door and they all stepped into the room. It was dark inside, as evening was falling, but when Deirdre flicked on the light, there was the strangest contraption Gus had ever seen. It shone golden in the middle of the room. The thing was around a metre and a half high and made of metal and glass. It had discs and cylinders, boxes and orbs as well as cogs and wheels, and was like something out of science fiction, a truly mystifying article.

'*Voila!*' said Deirdre.

She flicked a switch on the side of the machine and it shuddered into life, humming and clicking and whirring like something visiting from out of space.

'My father's movie projector. Practically a *curiosity* in some people's eyes. Nothing digital about *this* place.'

Gus's eyes bugged out of their sockets. She inched further into the room. The others made polite noises of 'wow' and 'cool'. She could tell they didn't get it. Gus however felt spangle-y inside, as though she might burst out of her skin. She moved around the table to get a view of the thing from all angles. The machine intrigued her, though she had no idea how it worked, or if they would be staying long enough to see it in action. Given her mother's track record, they would be on the road again in no time, she thought sadly.

'I've *no* idea how to *operate* it — the projector was my *father's* domain,' Deirdre was saying. 'It takes thirty-five-millimetre film, analogue stuff, *you* know. We're not *online* here. But I think the film can be screened in one go without changing reels these days. There's a *manual* around here *somewhere*, I recall. You *are* literate, I assume?'

Gus realised this last part was directed at her. 'I can read,' she assured Deirdre.

She was surprised to find herself wanting this job.

Stacked on a table beside the projector were round metal cases, some with film poking out. Gus recognised the stuff from art class at her last school, when their teacher had spent a few lessons showing them how photography had been done in the olden days.

Beyond the movie projector, a row of metal cabinets stood against the wall. One of the cabinet doors was ajar and Gus could see it was stuffed with more canisters of film.

On the opposite wall was a window covered by dusty peach-coloured curtains. She pulled one aside a little and saw it overlooked the drive-in, the concrete slabs for the cars and the speaker posts and the giant screen which looked like a big blank page without a story.

Gus felt a pang looking at the piles of film strewn haphazardly about. The place was sad, abandoned. She felt an urge to tidy up, set things right again. There were so many movies in here. So many hours she could while away, and pretend the outside world, and all of the people who wanted their mother's help, didn't exist.

Deirdre's voice cut through her thoughts again. '*Well*, do you think you're *up* for the job as *head projectionist*?'

Gus nodded. She would give it a go for as long as they had here. She couldn't wait to explore the stories in the tins. Deirdre had been right. This was the job that would suit her best.

Their mother cleared her throat. 'Miss Cronk, I don't know how to thank you.'

She sounded nervous to go on, but Gus could tell she wanted to say something else.

'You're *welcome*, Delphine,' the other woman replied, ushering them out of the projection room and back down the stairs to the cafe. 'The drive-in has been empty these past two months ever since my father's … *tragic disappearance*. I simply *couldn't* get staff fit to work under my *leadership*. It's *wonderful* we'll be re-opening soon. We've all got *bills* to pay! I've no idea why the locals have been staying away, as I'm *more* than capable of putting on a good show. I'm *hoping* you'll have better luck. I don't expect your work to be up to *my* standard as you're *new* to the industry but *modest* profit margins for the time being will *suffice*. Do you think that's within *reach*?'

'I hope so, Miss Cronk.'

'Good,' said Deirdre, decisively. She turned business-like. 'Movies are screened from Friday to Sunday evenings, rain, hail or *shine*. Let's *see*, tomorrow is Saturday, so you have practically a *week* to get up to speed and operational.'

'Great,' their mother said, sounding distracted.

'It's agreed then,' Deirdre said, smiling. 'You're the new Starlight *caretakers*. It's only *temporary*, mind. I *do* wish I could offer you a longer lease, but this is an, er, *interim* arrangement *only*.'

She lowered her voice to a stage whisper. 'It will be *just* until my father's last will and testament is finalised. Some legal items, *you know*, to straighten out. Clarification around my father's, er, *status*. Apparently, I have to make a *court* application to fast-track the death certificate. After all I've *suffered*. And as if the place *wouldn't* be passed on to me to do with as I see *fit*! The only surviving *heir*.'

'Oh,' said their mother, her shoulders drooping.

Gus was glad someone understood what Deirdre was talking about. Did she imagine it, or did her mother seem disappointed they wouldn't be staying here for long?

'I have *plans* for this place,' Deirdre said mysteriously, 'and I intend to get started the *moment* the will is executed. But then, I suppose a short-term arrangement will suit you, Delphine, given, your er, *situation*.'

She gestured at their overstuffed car, filled with all their worldly belongings.

'Yes,' their mother said, blinking and taking a step back from Deirdre.

Alice crossed her arms.

Deirdre stuck out her hand and their mother hesitated only slightly before she took it. They shook solemnly.

Mrs Able cleared her throat. 'Er, and um, about the lodgings, Miss Cronk? You mentioned accommodation was part of the deal on the phone.'

She had worked up the nerve to say it. Deirdre let out a peal of laughter, a sound befitting a silver screen starlet. 'Oh of *course*, Delphine, I nearly *forgot*,' she said. 'Silly *me*. You can all stay in the *caravan*. It's just behind the cafe.' She pointed vaguely to a footpath running around the building. 'An original Happy Camper. It is a two-bedder *really*, but it'll be so ... *cosy* with the four of you. I'm *sure* you're used to bunking in together, well, due to your *circumstances*.'

Alice narrowed her eyes.

'Caravan?' echoed their mother, a panicked look on her face.

'*Yes*, dear,' confirmed Deirdre. 'You'll *love* it. All vinyl interiors. Original kitchenette to *boot*.'

Mrs Able's mouth opened but words did not come out.

Deirdre turned business-like again. 'Right. I'm *off*. Help yourself to anything in the Moonbeam freezer for *dinner*. The local school is in *walking distance* and the children can start on Monday. I recommend Calvary Convenience Store for *supplies*, where I have a grocery

45

account for the Moonbeam you may *charge to*. Note, I will review this *weekly* for *anomalies*. And *steer clear* of the bowling alley — rough crowd, *you* know. Rehearsals for *Les Mis* start on *Tuesday*, so I will be *very* busy, but I suppose you *could* call my *landline* at my home in town, if you need assistance with anything.'

She paused for breath.

'Caravan?' repeated their mother.

She was looking pale, Gus thought.

'Yes,' Deirdre said, a bit impatiently. 'Any *further* questions?' asked the Director of the Amateur Dramatic Society as she climbed into the driver's seat of her car.

'Um, what about the drycleaning?' asked Alice, pointing to *The Starlight Drive-In Movie Theatre (and drycleaners)* sign.

'Oh *that*,' said Deirdre, dismissively. 'If anyone asks about that, just direct them to *me*.'

With that, she started her sedan again and tooted the horn, gaily. '*Goodbye*, Able family,' she said cheerily. 'I'll see *you* on Friday night for the grand re-opening!'

Chapter 5

Inside the caravan it smelled of wee and mould. Their mother said it was likely a family of possums had inhabited it for a time. Gus hoped she was right and that that time was over.

Space was also tight in the caravan. The interior consisted of a double bed with a single bunk above it and a tiny kitchenette, and the decor was entirely brown and orange. There was a small TV mounted on the wall, but it was definitely not a smart one. Gus groaned inwardly as she recalled what Deirdre had said about the lack of internet here. How would Gus be able to read stories now? She was probably banned from libraries across the country for stealing *Matilda*; she imagined some sinister database of offenders failing to return books with her name right at the top of the list. Without internet, she couldn't even read e-books. At their last house she'd at least read the stories she borrowed at night under the covers on Troy's cracked tablet, which he'd won in a bet at the pub. Perhaps, she consoled herself, she could borrow books from the library at the local school they would soon be attending.

There wasn't a toilet or shower inside the caravan either. The Ables had to use the public toilet-block ones behind the cafe, to be shared with the drive-in patrons on movie nights.

On their first night at the Starlight, after a dinner of sausage rolls and frozen peas, the three Able kids had squashed together in the double bed. Their mother had insisted.

'I'll be fine in the single,' she assured them.

She turned on her side above them and sighed deeply. It did not sound like a sigh of contentment.

Squashed between her sister and brother that first evening, Gus tried to get comfortable. She needed to pee and Alice's elbow was poking her in the ribs, while Artie was twirling a piece of Gus's hair in his sleep. Gus tried not to think watery thoughts and fretted about the new school she would be attending soon. Who would be her teacher? What would they put in their school lunches? And how would she avoid making friends?

Miserably, Gus rose and climbed over the sleeping forms of her brother and sister, unlocked the door to the caravan and tiptoed down the steps. It was raining again and she ran to the shower block, avoiding the puddles as best she could.

The security light came on as she entered and she tried not to look up as a possum — or something worse — scurried across the roof. She was just drying her hands on her pyjamas when she heard it, a noise like the scraping of a chair over floorboards.

The noise sounded like it was coming from the projection room above the cafe. Gus stood in the doorway of the toilet block and glanced up through the misting rain towards the window overlooking the drive-in.

The projection room curtains were open, and she saw a lamp had been turned on. Gus froze as she made out a figure pacing back and forth.

Someone was in the projection room.

Gus felt something tread up her spine. She strained to get a better look through the rain.

The person was thin with a little belly and walked in a slightly hunched way as they strode back and forth. Whoever it was wore what looked to be a fishing hat. They appeared to be tinkering with the old projector. The projector lens blinked like an eye fluttering open from sleep. A beam of light was trained on the great white screen.

She shivered and it wasn't because of the rainy night.

Gus forced herself to walk back to the caravan without looking at the main building again, though she could feel the presence in the projection room was still there, behind her.

When she got back to the caravan, she opened the door with shaking hands and snuck back under the covers. She heard her mother trying to stifle her crying. She needn't have worried. Artie was snoring and even Alice had dropped off, still pretty as she slept.

Gus's mind whirred, the image of the intruder playing over and over in her mind like a film skipping. She made lists to distract herself and finally fell asleep pondering: *How not to make friends at school on Monday.*

Chapter 6

The next day, feeling rumpled all over, Gus begged to stay behind at the drive-in while Artie, Alice and her mum piled into the Camry.

They were heading into Calvary to rummage the op shops for second-hand shoes and school uniforms.

That morning, after a breakfast of odd-shaped pancakes, made from an only slightly out of date mix, their mother had sat them around one of the picnic tables in the Moonbeam and outlined her hazy plan.

'You heard Deirdre — I mean Miss Cronk. We're all going to have to pitch in,' she began. 'First we need to jazz this place up. Clean up the buildings and tidy the grounds so the drive-in looks inviting. Then we're going to get the locals coming back. We need them to buy movie tickets and food from the Moonbeam.'

'They'll need to buy a lot of movies and meal deals, though, won't they? Before we even break even, let alone make a modest profit margin?' Alice replied. 'Deirdre said we get twenty per cent of the ticket sales. How many tickets will we need to sell, exactly?'

Her sister looked worried. Alice hadn't smiled since they'd arrived, Gus thought. And it had probably been way before that too. Gus couldn't actually recall the last time she'd seen Alice smile.

'I haven't done the maths yet,' their mother said uncertainly.

Alice's shoulders sagged.

'But I will,' their mother said, putting a hand on Alice's shoulder. 'I'll add up costs for food and ... and power and everything, so we charge enough to make a profit. It's a good idea, Alice, thank you. Any other ideas to get the punters in?' she asked looking around the table at the family.

'Maybe we could get a dinosaur?' suggested Artie. 'And put it right by the front gate! A mechanical one, this big, that roars.' He roared in demonstration and nearly fell off his seat.

'I'll look into it, Artie,' said their mother, catching him.

'You made me leave my Transformers behind,' Artie reminded her.

He had a point, Gus thought.

'If we do a good job selling tickets maybe I can buy you a new one,' Mrs Able said. 'What do you think?'

'It's a deal,' said Artie, extending a sticky hand.

They shook on it.

'The main thing is,' their mother continued, 'we need to entice people to come back here. That way, we'll sell tickets and make some money. Then we just have to follow the recipes Miss Cronk left and choose good movies. Simple, right?'

There was silence around the table. She turned to her middle child. 'Gus, we'll have to start thinking about the first movie we'll screen. Something popular, that people will want to see.'

Gus nodded, though her tummy was dancing. She had no idea where to start.

'If we do this right and get some money coming in, I can pay back what I owe Troy,' their mother said. 'I can get the car returned or buy it from him. And then we're off the hook. We're free.'

She made a gesture with her hands as though releasing a bird, like a magician might.

'To make that happen though, we need return business. Regulars, don't we?' Alice asked, her forehead creased.

'You're right, Alice. I need to think about how we can do that. In business, that's called having a strategy. I just remembered that from uni.' She paused, then said softly, gazing around at the drive-in and the canefields beyond, 'It's kind of beautiful, here, don't you think? I mean, it could be. If we put the work in.'

Then her face went serious. 'But we have to keep my old job a secret. OK? At least until things are sorted with the car and everything. We don't want anyone to hear about what I did, in case Troy gets word of it and comes looking for us. Does everyone understand? Arthur? Augusta? Alice?'

She looked at the children in turn.

The three of them nodded, though Alice broke her mother's gaze and looked away.

'Good. Do you understand what this means for us? It's a fresh start. A chance to begin over in a new place,' Mrs Able said.

Later, as Gus stood in the driveway beside the sky-blue car and her family piled into it, she had to agree. There was something about this place that drew her in.

The pull to explore the Starlight was strong. The land was so different from the grey skies and jammed-in buildings of the city. Here it was sunny and open. You could throw your head back and see the whole of the blue sky.

'Hop in, Gus,' her mother said. 'We have to get going. Everything closes at lunchtime on Saturday in towns like this.'

She watched the others do up their seatbelts. Alice helped Artie with his.

'Please can I stay here, Mum?' Gus asked.

Her mother turned her head to one side, a sure sign she was going to say no.

'I can start tidying up the place,' Gus said quickly before Delphine could speak. She gestured to the drive-in grounds. There were weeds covering the cement slabs where the cars parked to watch films. Litter and fallen branches were strewn around the screen. The place looked like it had been abandoned for some time. 'There's so much to do before we open on Friday,' she added.

Her mother hesitated, then shrugged. 'All right. I suppose you're old enough to be left on your own for a little while,' Mrs Able said. 'But stay within the drive-in grounds and don't talk to any strangers, OK?'

'I won't,' Gus assured her.

'We'll be back in an hour or so,' her mother said, putting the car into gear. 'Rubbish bags are under the Moonbeam sink,' she called as they drove away.

After waving them off, Gus dutifully fetched a rubbish bag and began to pick up litter. As she worked, her gaze drifted to the screen. It was covered in mildew and bird poo and would have to be scrubbed clean before they showed any movies. As she gazed up at the blank white space, it seemed a miracle of sorts, how stories were brought to life up there, against the fetching backdrop of the sky.

Gus couldn't say why she liked this place so much, and wanted to explore every part of the drive-in. Everywhere else seemed so, so *un-Starlight-like*, in comparison. Although she wasn't sure about going into the projection room, especially after last night. Especially alone.

She tried to turn her thoughts back to litter patrol and away from the presence she had seen. Don't be silly, Gus told herself. There hadn't been anyone in the projection room last night. She must have imagined it. Had she dreamed it, perhaps?

Still, the image of the person pacing lingered in her mind and she felt uneasy.

Gus wondered if seeing this kind of thing was what made her mother so jittery and had all of them running, causing an Able exodus from every place they had tried to anchor. It wasn't just talking to people's dead relatives, she knew. The gift had lots of different shapes and faces. She shuddered as she imagined who or what might have chased her mother in the past. Her mind conjured faceless ghosts, a flash of a no-longer-human form, unable to be made out, but always there, a nebulous spiky presence at her back.

And it hadn't just been Mum, Gran had it too.

Gus remembered when Gran had got sick. It had only been a few years earlier when the scary text messages had started. Gran was living a few suburbs away from them in the city and was being visited by ill-meaning spirits, she claimed. They wanted things from her. They wanted her to do things for them, bad things. To escape them, Gran disappeared for a while, living rough. She had returned home after months away, looking bedraggled and toting a one-eyed cat, as well as plastic shopping bags filled entirely with other bags.

She'd been admitted to a kind of hospital after that. At the clinic, her visitations were managed by pink and blue pills, swallowed twice a day with weak tea. Gran was forced to watch soaps on TV and do crafts with hideous-coloured yarns. Her gift had been too much for her, Gus overheard her mother murmur to a nurse on one of their visits. The nurse had looked alarmed, as though she might start administering pills to their mum, too.

On that visit, as they'd been about to leave, Gran had seized their mother's arm and whispered, 'Protect the girls from it, Delphine, whatever you do.'

Her mother had nodded, tears in her eyes. She had gathered Gran's latest craft project and quickly ushered the children out the door.

That day, it had felt to Gus like she was losing Gran, the only person who had ever understood her. Gran was slowly drifting away on a boat out to sea.

Stop it, Gus told herself. Gran was better now — she had learned to manage her gift and eased off the pills. She avoided places where restless souls roamed and also people who might try and use her gifts for dark intents. She had found peace on her farm, in her shack by the sea. Though she wished they had gone to see Gran on this trip, she didn't want to bring her more troubles. And the Ables were safe in Calvary, weren't they? There was too much sunshine here to let ghosts in.

She saw she had almost filled her rubbish bag, so she lugged it to the council bin and retrieved another from the Moonbeam's kitchen. She planned to collect all the takeaway wrappers and plastic bottles and cans piled around the screen. It seemed liked trespassers had been using the site as their own personal playground since Mr Cronk, the former projectionist, had passed on. At least they could return the bottles and cans to their local recycling depot and make some extra cash.

She was about to head over to the movie screen when, from under the awning of the Moonbeam Cafe, Gus was startled to see a boy standing by one of the tall posts that supported it. She froze on the spot and made a peep of surprise.

The boy clocked Gus too and stared back at her for a moment. He had red hair, which was cut short and combed neatly all over. He looked to be about her age or a little older and was wearing a checked shirt and jeans, as well as old brown boots, though it was warm in the sun.

Her heart beating fast, Gus called, 'Excuse me. This is private property.'

The boy continued to look in her direction, as though considering how to reply.

'You can't be here,' Gus said, a little louder this time.

The boy shrugged and loped off in the direction of the road, towards the canefields beyond the drive-in.

Chapter 7

On her first day at Calvary Primary Gus stood at the front of her new class, the other students a blur of unfamiliar faces.

Her second-hand uniform itched, and the shoes their mother had dug up at the local charity shop were way too tight. Sweat trickled down her armpits and behind her knees, pooling in her school socks. She hoped nobody saw. '

Her teacher's name was Ms McKenzie and she seemed nice, in a cat-lady sort of way. Ms McKenzie wore a skirt with a variety of cats printed all over it and a cat brooch was pinned to her pussy-bow blouse. Even her tortoiseshell glasses were in the shape of a cat's eyes.

'Good morning, class,' Ms McKenzie said in a singsong voice. 'Today we have a new student. Her name is Augusta Able.'

There were sniggers from the back of the class. Gus cringed. She opened her mouth, but all that came out was a squeak.

More sniggers from the back, while a few kids laughed openly.

'Can you repeat that please, Augusta?' the teacher asked pleasantly.

'It's Gus,' she managed to say.

The class outright guffawed in unison.

'Class!' said Ms McKenzie clapping her hands to indicate they should settle down. 'Gus, would you like to tell us a bit about where you came from?' she coaxed. 'Perhaps a bit about home?'

Gus cringed again. This was not an easy question to answer. Did Ms McKenzie mean her last city and school, or the place before that? She could list half a dozen places and not be sure any of them was *home*. Or did her new teacher mean the place where Gus was born and had lived for her early years when things weren't so bad for them, or for their mother? Or Gran's place, where Gus felt most like herself?

Where you came from was a question like one of those complex maths problems, Gus thought, the kind where you had to keep dividing things, breaking them up into smaller and smaller parts until they were minute, so tiny they became insignificant. Gus hadn't ever had a proper answer, although every teacher at every new school had asked the question.

Mercifully, she had prepared something earlier. That morning she had stood in front of the mottled bathroom mirror in the drive-in toilet block and practised her response to this question. She knew from prior experience standing in front of other classrooms and other new faces that this would be a passable answer. She took a deep breath and began. 'I came from down south. It's colder there and the buildings are taller. The sun doesn't get in as much. Before that, we lived on a stone-fruit farm. Cherries are a lot of work.'

She knew how much information to give and how much to leave out. This was something she knew from experience. Still, it didn't make it any easier to speak. The lines caught in her throat, like a bit of foul medicine. 'I live with my mum and my sister, Alice, and my brother, Arthur,' she continued. 'At the moment, we're staying at the Starlight Drive-In Movie Theatre (and drycleaners).'

There was a sharp intake of breath. Gus looked around. Gradually the individual students came into focus. There were the usual suspects, a trio of boys in striped socks and footy boots, with pink cheeks and cowlicks, as well as a quartet of girls wearing lip gloss, their long hair centre parted. These were the ones who always claimed Alice for their gang, her shiny hair marking her as one of their own.

Another girl, skinny, with inky-dark hair, in a faded uniform, who obviously did not belong to the lip-gloss clique, was looking at Gus wide-eyed, mouth agape. A couple of the boys had raised eyebrows too. The students obviously thought she was weird. Or poor, for living at the drive-in, which was both true and worse than being weird in terms of the playground hierarchy.

Stop talking now, Gus thought, and mumbled, 'Anyway, that's all.'

'Thank you, Augusta — I mean Gus. You may take a seat,' said Ms McKenzie. 'Now, take out your science textbooks, class. Today we're going to learn about comets.'

There was a collective groan from the class. It was music to Gus's ears. She slunk over to an unoccupied desk in the third row, next to the gaping dark-haired girl.

'You can look at my textbook with me if you like,' said the girl.

'Thanks,' Gus muttered, grateful for the kindness.

'I'm Nicole,' the girl said, smiling. She had one front tooth shorter than all the rest, as though it had quit growing halfway through. Gus liked her straight away and scooted closer to her desk.

Ms McKenzie clapped her hands excitedly. 'Now, class,' their teacher said, 'we are about to be visited by a septuagenarian in our skies. Riley's Comet is a short-period comet, meaning it appears in our hemisphere's sky every seventy years or so. This makes it possible to see it twice in one lifetime — for some lucky individuals.'

A hand shot up, belonging to one of the footy boys.

'Yes, Ralph?' said the teacher.

'My dad said this place attracts comets. He reckons Riley's is headed straight for us.' Ralph drew a finger across his neck, the implications of his gesture clear.

The teacher nodded. 'I understand some local people do believe the comet is a prophecy of death, not unlike those living in the time of the plague.' She cleared her throat. 'Modern *science* however tells us Riley's is a celestial object that will be visible to the naked eye in winter. June is only a month away …'

The footy boys tittered at the word 'naked'. As Gus looked around, she saw that most of the class had zoned out. Only Nicole appeared to be listening.

The lesson laboured by. As the teacher droned on about matter and ice particles and tails, Gus tried to shrink into her uniform and not breathe too loudly. Nicole followed the lesson in the textbook with her pointer finger.

'Do you think this will be on the test?' the girl whispered to Gus anxiously.

'I'm not sure,' Gus replied.

'What do you have for lunch?' Nicole asked then.

'Um, a ham sandwich, I think,' said Gus, trying to recall what her mother had shoved at her in tin foil as she'd bundled the children out of the caravan door.

'Ugh,' said Nicole. 'Is it free-range ham? Or home-killed?'

'Um, I don't think it's either,' Gus replied honestly.

She knew full well it had been on special at the cut-price store deli.

'Well, I won't be able to sit too close to you at lunch,' Nicole informed her. 'I am allergic to anything processed with nitrates. I have a seaweed salad today. You can try some if you want,' she offered. 'And I also have green juice with ginger in it.'

'Sounds great,' Gus said weakly.

'So don't forget, class,' Ms McKenzie's voice cut in. 'Your group research assignment is on Riley's Comet. There'll be a prize at the end of the term for the most accurate representation of a comet, and I'll be entering that first-place assignment into the state-wide science competition.'

Nicole flipped through the chapter of the science text, frowning.

'Miss, that isn't in the book,' she called out. 'Riley's Comet isn't in here.'

Ms McKenzie smiled. 'The best things are rarely in textbooks, Nicole. For this project you'll have to do some of your own research,' the teacher said.

'But—' said Nicole.

She was cut off by the bell. The students rose and poured into the yard. Nicole and Gus were caught up in the tide and propelled out of the door with the rest of the kids.

'Where should we start our research, do you think?' Nicole fretted at Gus's shoulder. 'There probably won't even be a free computer at the library right now. They get booked out at lunchtime, even though they're from the dark ages. And what's a septa-whatever anyway?'

Nicole didn't seem to need an answer to her questions, and though Gus tried to drift away from her classmate, Nicole followed her as they retrieved their lunch, prattling away until they were both somehow sitting together on an unclaimed aluminium bench in the sun. Nicole unwrapped her lunch and began to eat. Gus looked at the other girl's food doubtfully.

'It's both low GI and macrobiotic,' Nicole explained.

Gus chewed her ham sandwich and reflected she had no idea what Nicole was talking about. She wondered if Nicole actually did either.

As Gus ate and nodded at Nicole's steady stream of chatter, she wondered when it would be time to go home and explore the drive-in again. She told herself it was time to brave the projection room. It would be broad daylight, after all.

She caught sight of Alice in the yard. Her sister sat only a few benches away, also eating her sandwich, surrounded by a cluster of students already. A group sat around her, a halo of footy boys and lip-gloss-wearing types like the ones in her own class, but taller and better looking.

Gus looked for the red-haired boy she had seen at the drive-in on her first day, but he wasn't there. Alice smiled at whatever it was her new friends were saying. Alice was having a very different first day from Gus's. Like always, Gus thought.

'Gus? Earth to Gus. You can have some of my seaweed if you like,' Nicole was saying.

Gus politely declined, but Nicole insisted. As Gus took a piece and tried to swallow it, she watched her sister throw her head back. Alice was laughing at something one of her new friends was saying, her hair glowing like corn-silk in the sun.

Chapter 8

Gus trudged a little behind her brother and sister on the way home from school.

Artie too seemed to have enjoyed his first day and chattered to Alice about playing wall ball with the whole class at lunch. Apparently, he had been the last man standing.

As they approached the Starlight, Gus saw the place looked less dingy than it had on their first arrival in the rain last Friday. Tufts of green grass poked through the bald patches of the drive-in car space surfaces. The large screen dominating the site looked freshly washed from the rain. There was no sign of the trespasser from Saturday.

They straggled into the cafe kitchen, where their mother was practising recipes from the book Deirdre had given her, and tossed aside their schoolbags. There was a burned smell hanging in the air. Recipes were laid out all over the benches.

'How's it going, Mum?' Gus ventured.

Their mother's apron was spattered with food. She wore a hairnet from which her wild salt and pepper curls were escaping. 'Don't ask,' Mrs Able muttered. 'Do you think I can substitute yogurt for mayonnaise?'

'Not a good idea, Mum,' Gus said.

Alice grabbed some flavoured milk from the fridge and sat down with Artie to help him with his Year One reading homework at one of the aluminium tables. Gus grabbed a packet of salt and vinegar chips, squared her shoulders, and escaped up the steps to the projection room. She had looked forward to checking out the films in the silver canisters ever since Deirdre had showed them around. With the other Able family members occupied for the afternoon, now was the perfect time. She would have to brave it, and she felt better that her family would be just downstairs, in case of anything lurking. Besides, there wasn't a lot of time to waste. They were supposed to re-open the Starlight on Friday, after all.

Inside the projection room it was dim, so Gus pushed open the peach curtains. Dust motes were flung about like downy stars. Daylight struggled through the dirty windows and into the room, illuminating the curiosity hulking in the room, which Gus had been thinking about all day.

She approached the projector and touched it tentatively. She had expected it to be warm, humming under her hands, but it was cool. Whoever had been there the other night had not left the machine on. More proof it was a dream, she told herself.

Gus moved to the old metal cabinets where the reels of film were stored. Plumes of dust rose from the carpet as she walked. The place needed a good tidy-up that was for sure. She would see if she could find a vacuum cleaner in the cafe storeroom later.

She took her time rifling through cardboard boxes in which the reels of film were stored, each in its own silver canister. The boxes seemed to be loosely organised by genre: one held cartoons, while another was full of comedies. Another was labelled *Romance* while another box read *Fantasy*. Each silver canister was labelled with the film title in felt-tip pen on masking tape. She reached for one called *The NeverEnding Story*. Was it any good? The title sounded a tad drawn out to her. Intrigued, she prised the lid off the tin.

'And just what are you planning on doing with that, missy?' came a voice from behind her.

Gus dropped the tin like it was on fire. It fell to the floor, bursting open, and lengths of negative unspooled everywhere. It was definitely a never-ending roll of film. She whirled to face the intruder. It felt like her heart was in her throat.

Standing in the doorway was a man who looked to be in his seventies, wearing denim shorts, a zip-up spray jacket and a terry-towelling fishing hat. His knees were wrinkled like an elephant's. His legs were skinny while his belly was generous. He had sun-weathered skin and blue eyes which right now were most certainly not twinkling.

'I'm sorry,' stammered Gus. 'I didn't mean to—'

'Who are you?' the man thundered.

'I'm Gus,' she stammered. 'Gus Able. My family are staying at the drive-in.'

'Well, Gus, that's news to me. I would have thought I'd be the first to know.'

'I'm s-sorry. I j-just, um ...' Gus stammered. She tried again. 'It's just, Deirdre said we could stay.

I mean, Miss Cronk? She asked us to, in fact. At the interview?'

'Deirdre? She said you could stay? What interview?' the man demanded.

'For the job. Running the drive-in?' Gus replied.

The man looked at her blankly.

'My mum is in charge of the cafe, my sister looks after the ticket booth and my brother is the general dogsbody.'

'*Deirdre* brought you here to run this place? *My* Deirdre?'

'Yes,' Gus said fearfully. 'And I'm, um, to be the projectionist.'

'Is that so?' the man replied, appearing to be an equal mix of outraged and amused.

'Um, yes?' Gus said. 'And may I ask who you are?'

'I'm Henry,' harrumphed the man. 'That's Mr Cronk to you.'

Gus gasped. Was this Deirdre's dear departed father? Was she talking with a *ghost*?

The idea was terrifying and ridiculous and exhilarating all at the same time. It sometimes happened to people in stories. And one or two other people she knew. People Gus was in fact related to.

She realised she was holding her breath. She had goosebumps all over and the hairs on her arms and legs were raised like tentacles.

'And you have a lot of experience handling film, have you?' Henry was asking.

Her heart danced an irregular beat in her chest. 'Sure,' Gus said slowly, backing away. 'I mean, I watch TV sometimes.'

You have to get out of here, her brain told her body. But she felt trapped in the room, perhaps by the force of the ghost's presence.

'Humph! I knew it. You're totally unqualified for the role.'

Wait, was he insulting her? If Henry Cronk was a ghost, he was kind of a grumpy one. That made her feel less frightened for a moment. Still, it wouldn't do to anger him more. She had seen first-hand how situations like this could turn bad. Gus had to act like this was normal. She swallowed her fear like it was cough syrup.

'I was thinking of screening this,' she said holding up the empty canister. 'Do you think it will get people in?'

He seemed not to hear her. 'What was Deirdre thinking?' Henry muttered to himself.

'I — I guess not, then,' Gus said.

She felt a weight in her chest and hung her head. Henry, or his ghost anyway, was right. She had no idea how to operate the projector, though she had been looking forward to figuring out how it worked. It had promised hours of delicious absorption, away from her family and people who might want to be her friends.

'I can't believe my daughter. Letting an amateur in here!' Henry fumed. 'Typical Deirdre, interfering in my business again. And as far as she's concerned, my grave's not even cold.'

Gus remembered what Deirdre had said about the argument she had with Henry before he had disappeared, about the Power of Eternity or something. They were awful terms for a father and daughter to end on. It was like something from a tragic story.

To her surprise, Gus felt tears charging up her throat, clogging her nose and springing leaks in her eyes. Snot bubbled from her nostrils and she started, of all things, to cry.

The ghost of Henry Cronk looked appalled. 'Stop that,' he said. 'Stop snivelling, will you?'

'I'm sorry,' sniffed Gus. 'It's just that—' She couldn't get the words out. She felt an overwhelming urge to tell Henry about everything, including their long drive to escape the city and the pale woman at the petrol station. Then there was the odd girl with seaweed for lunch at school, as well as the fact they were living in a *caravan*. Being a projectionist had seemed like the one cool thing she had, and now a ghost had shown up to claim his job back.

But she didn't know where to begin with any of it. And anyway, why would the ghost of Mr Cronk even care? She began to sob-hiccup.

'It's all right, child,' Henry said, sounding alarmed now. 'Please don't cry,' he pleaded. 'I didn't mean to upset you.'

'I *know*,' Gus wailed.

'Ssshhhh, child, please. We don't want to draw any attention to ourselves. Deirdre might hear you.'

'She's gone back to town,' Gus snuffled.

The ghost relaxed visibly. 'Just as well. Look, I'm sorry, er — what did you say your name was again?'

'Gus,' she sniffled.

'Look, Gus, perhaps I was a bit gruff, out of the gate. You're only a kid. It's just, I've been the Starlight's head projectionist for over fifty years. I'm a bit territorial, I suppose. You can't blame me for that.'

'It's OK,' Gus hiccupped.

But it wasn't. She wondered why she was so upset about not having the projector to herself. The feeling alarmed her even more than the fact that she was currently in the presence of a ghost. She wiped her nose on her sleeve and tried to stifle the sobs threatening to burst from her chest.

'Now I've gone and done it,' Henry sighed, regarding her. 'I guess I'll *have* to show you how it works.'

'Oh no, that's OK,' Gus began.

His sudden kindness was setting her off again. Besides, she didn't really want to be in close proximity to him. She suppressed a wail.

'I insist,' said Henry. 'For upsetting you. Besides, we can't let this place go to wrack and ruin, now, can we?'

Gus had to agree. She liked the Starlight too much already.

'No,' she peeped.

'So let's pick up that film and get to work,' Henry said.

She retrieved *The NeverEnding Story* from the floor.

'Thank you,' sobbed Gus. 'The Starlight is re-opening on Friday and I have no idea what to do with this thing.'

'That soon?'

Gus nodded.

'That's Deirdre for you. Onwards and upwards. Well, we don't have much time. But I can teach you the basics,' Henry said.

Hope surged through her as he said this.

The projectionist continued. 'First things first. Have you thought about what you'll screen? Have you advertised in the local paper?'

Gus shook her head.

Henry sighed again. 'We're in worse shape than I thought.'

'Oh no,' said Gus, crushed all over again.

'Never mind,' Henry said quickly.

He was probably afraid Gus would start bawling again.

'We'll do the best we can with what we've got,' Henry said sounding resigned. 'Once more unto the breach, and all that.'

Gus looked at him, confused.

'It's from *Henry V*. By Shakespeare?' Henry explained.

Gus shook her head again.

Henry shrugged and moved on. 'Never mind. Let's talk projection. The first thing you need to understand is, light is king.'

He moved to the machine and indicated Gus should turn it on. She obliged by flicking the power switch. Henry pointed to the part that reminded Gus of an eye.

'This is the lens,' he explained. 'My trusty Xenon lamp, or light source inside this box —' here he indicated the projector's case '— illuminates the image on the film and casts it onto the big screen out there.'

He pointed to the white screen looming over the drive-in. Gus nodded that she understood — sort of.

'Now, these are the spools,' Henry continued, with one hand hovering over each of the machine's large wheels. 'These are what we feed the film into. Since the upgrade I made in the eighties to my father's trusty thirty-five-mil Kalee — the original projector when we opened the place — we can do a whole film in one go. No changeover, see?'

Gus nodded again. Henry looked as though he wasn't convinced, but continued with his instruction.

'The take-up spool is just as important as the feed spool, you see. Do you understand what I am saying, Gus? All of the parts are important. If one isn't working, the machine won't work either.'

It was all so technical. Gus hadn't expected screening movies to be so hard, but she nodded again anyway. She hoped she would understand how the projector worked by Friday. She couldn't be picky about her instructor, even if he was a ghost. She would worry about that part later. Right now, Gus needed all the help she could get.

Chapter 9

'So, what's it like, living at a deserted drive-in?' Nicole asked.

Gus and her science partner were sitting together at lunch again. The aluminium bench, hot from the noon sun, had seared their legs when they sat down. Calvary was the most northern and the most warm place Gus had ever been.

Gus shrugged at the question. She didn't know Nicole well enough to confide that her mother was playing fast and loose with the Moonbeam Cafe recipes or that she herself was being trained in movie projection by a ghost.

Around them, the other students were embroiled in complicated-looking social interactions. It seemed to Gus they knew automatically who to sit beside and who to pass notes to, as well as who to play handball with, and who to stay away from. It all seemed so easy to them, this business of friendship.

'Isn't it kind of spooky living there?' Nicole prompted.

Gus's science partner was speaking through a mouthful of what looked like raw fish. Gus had declined Nicole's offer to share lunch again, feigning a tummy ache. Her own lunch, a leftover sausage roll, sat untouched in the lunch box sitting beside her.

The tummy ache wasn't a complete lie. She had been feeling weird about meeting Henry all last night. She had contemplated telling her mum about the fact that oops, she could see ghosts too, apparently. Then she recalled how desperate her mother had been to escape that life. Memories tumbled through her mind, like her mother crying in the lounge room at her reading table. Unhappy families banging their fists on the door at midnight wanting answers. Angry spirits unable to give them. Her mother's door closed to them and the muffled sound of crying.

And now Gus had it too, the Able inheritance. Passed down from mother to daughter, Gran to Mum to Gus. It must have skipped Alice, she reflected. Her sister hadn't mentioned any encounter with Henry or anyone else of a spectral nature.

She had been distracted in class today too. Luckily, Ms McKenzie had continued enthusing about comets for practically the entire lesson.

Gus let out a squeak, a football was headed their way. She had just enough time to duck but the ball hit Nicole on the side of the head. Gus gasped and retrieved the ball from where it had rolled under their bench. 'Nicole! Are you OK?'

'Yeah,' said Nicole, rubbing the spot. 'I'm fine.' She shook her head a little, as though trying to regain her sense of balance and vision.

'Got you that time, Kale Girl!' shouted one of the footy boys from across the playground.

'Wait,' said Gus, 'did he just call you *Kale Girl*? Was that *deliberate*?'

'It's best not to react,' Nicole replied, her face closing down. 'It'll be over faster that way.'

The footy boy raced over and snatched the ball from Gus. 'Who's your loser friend, Kale Girl?' he asked, smirking first at Nicole and then at Gus.

'She's not my friend, Nathan. She's new and I'm just showing her the ropes,' Nicole said airily.

There was a red mark at Nicole's temple. As Gus stared at it, she felt her cheeks grow hot. Nathan shrugged and booted the ball back to his mates.

Gus continued to stare at Nicole. Was she really OK with what had just happened?

She watched the other girl take a bite of her lunch, wincing as she chewed. Gus felt a strange sensation, like a boiling feeling in her tummy. Nicole smiled though as if to reassure Gus she was fine and with effort Gus told herself to drop it, for now.

At least Nicole had clarified the friendship thing. Gus told herself it was a relief really, that Nicole didn't want to be friends either. It could have been awkward.

After a small silence, Nicole changed the subject. 'You can talk about it with me, you know,' she said. 'I won't tell anyone. I wouldn't like living in a haunted drive-in, either,' she added.

Gus sat up straight. Had she heard right? 'Wait. What did you just say?' How did Nicole know about the ghost in the projection room?

Nicole serenely took another bite of lunch. The raw fish she was eating looked to be covered in seeds and twigs. Gus hoped she wouldn't pass out from the sight.

'No wonder no one goes there any more,' Nicole said reasonably. 'I mean, why would anyone want to watch a movie with a *ghost* hanging around? In a *car*?'

She's speaking too loudly, Gus thought. She looked around desperately, but the other kids hadn't heard what Kale Girl had said. Nobody was paying them any attention. She breathed out in relief.

Gus's head was spinning, even though the part about watching a movie in a car seemed irrelevant. So, she had been correct. Henry the projectionist *was* a ghost. She got goosebumps on top of her goosebumps. Her head swam and her mouth ran dry.

Now she truly was her mother's daughter.

She felt stones collect in her throat, as big as the painted white ones that edged the path to the drive-in. She tried to swallow them down, but she couldn't.

Calm down, Gus, she told herself. Get the facts first. She slowed her breathing and painfully tried to swallow the stones. 'I thought he went missing?' she replied, with difficulty. 'Deirdre said ... Was his death, like, confirmed?'

'Well, good as,' said Nicole. 'He hasn't been seen alive for ages. There were missing person notices up in the fish and chip shop and everything. It was even on the news. Do you know, they reckon he haunts the projection room, above the cafe?'

Gus swallowed. 'I — I did not know that,' she said.

'People have reported seeing a figure in the window, moving back and forth. And,' Nicole continued, 'mid-movie he creeps up to your car when you least suspect it —' here she lowered her voice dramatically '— and he steals your popcorn!'

'Oh, my goodness,' Gus said. 'Really?'

'Yep. No one likes their snacks being stolen,' Nicole said knowingly. 'Especially by a dead person.'

'And everyone knows about this?' Gus enquired. 'Does the whole town know?'

'It's an open secret,' Nicole informed her.

Deirdre had neglected to mention this. Nor had it been included in the contract her mother had signed, Gus felt sure. She sat silently, pondering this development.

Nicole brushed a trace of seed and twig crumb from her lips. 'Speaking of not being seen in ages, that reminds me. The seventy-year-old comet, remember? We have to start our science assignment, or Ms McKenzie is going to crack it.'

Gus stared out at the yard. Perhaps she could ask her mother what to do about the ghost? Then she recalled how sad her job had made her. She didn't want to lump more on Mum's already full plate. She watched the other students jostling and playing and laughing, a blur of regular kids doing regular things. They're so lucky, she thought.

A perfectly still pair drew Gus's eye. In the far-right corner of the yard by the school fence she saw Alice talking to someone. Gus recognised the person as the tall red-haired boy she had seen on her first day at the Starlight.

Gus felt a pang of jealousy. Of course he was happy to stick around and talk to Alice. Everyone liked Alice. She was smarter than Gus, funnier and more confident. Even her hair was shinier. Alice was more, well, everything. Alice was sunny and bright, like the grass after rain. Gus was gloomy, more of an opaque puddle.

'Hello, earth to Gus,' Nicole was saying. 'We have to research Riley's Comet, remember? We are going to win that Mega-scope!'

Their teacher had let on that the prize for the best comet assignment in the state-wide competition was a special telescope made for viewing celestial matter, one big enough to be mounted in a public area for use by the whole town.

At that moment, as though he knew he was being watched, the red-haired boy looked over in her direction. He shocked Gus by giving a little wave. Seeing this, Alice turned and squinted at her. Realising who it was, Alice appeared to stare daggers at Gus. Alice called out something Gus didn't catch. Then she resumed her conversation. A few kids kicking a soccer ball nearby turned and stared at her sister.

'Gus? Come in, Gus!'

Nicole's voice was like a worm twisting in her ear. Gus tore her eyes away from her sister and the boy.

'I've been thinking, do you want to come over one afternoon next week, after school? How about Thursday? We can work on our science project together,' Nicole suggested.

This got Gus's attention. She hadn't been invited to anyone's house since — well — ever.

'You mean, you want me to come to your *house*?' She was so surprised she picked up her sausage roll and took a bite.

'Well, it's a townhouse, but yes my house,' Nicole confirmed. 'My mum is cool with it. She's going to make snacks while we brainstorm our project. I told my mum you eat gluten and dairy and a whole bunch of other foods from packets. She said it will be a challenge, but she'll see if she can make something catering to your, um, diet. Though she won't stoop to serving sugar,' Nicole finished up.

'OK,' said Gus, her head still reeling from the invitation. 'Well, thanks. That would be great.'

'My mum said it would be a good idea to invite you, seeing as nobody forced you to be my science partner. You're the first voluntary kid I've had over.'

So I'm not the only one, Gus thought. The part of Gus that kept her safe from this kind of trap piped up that she should decline the invitation. But another part of her whispered against all reason, *this time it might be OK.*

The boiling feeling in her stomach subsided. She would have to be careful they didn't become friends. That would be disastrous, especially now Gus had inherited whatever it was her mother had. This almost guaranteed they would have to move again. This was the reason Gus never made friends in the first place, it was too hard when they had to leave. While Nicole hadn't actually used the f-word, they *were* still going to hang out. Gus would have to be careful.

The bell rang. There was bedlam in the yard as the students frantically finished their last games, whispered their last secrets, or had their final bites of lunch. Gus and Nicole rose from their bench and began to walk back to class. Gus brushed sausage roll crumbs from her uniform.

In the far corner of the yard by the fence, she saw Alice and the boy had moved. There was no trace of either of them.

Nicole gave Gus her address and told Gus to meet her there next Thursday after school.

'I'd offer you a lift on our tandem bike, when Mum picks me up,' she said, 'but we've only got two helmets.'

'No worries,' Gus assured her science partner. 'I'll find my own way there.'

Chapter 10

That afternoon, still in her school uniform, Gus filled a bucket with soap and hot water. She found a ladder and long-handled broom in the cafe storeroom and tramped the gear over to the gigantic outdoor movie screen.

A smear of purple bat poo had fouled the surface. How were paying customers going to watch a movie with muck, not to mention layers of mildew, on the screen? Gus tried not to remember that she was yet to choose the movie for the grand re-opening. After what Nicole had said at school, the pressure was on to choose something that would lure locals out of their homes to visit a haunted drive-in.

She was on the next to last rung, dipping the broom in the bucket of suds, about to begin scrubbing off the bat poo, when a voice from below said, 'You should be careful up there.'

Gus wobbled on the ladder, almost losing her footing.

She peered down at the person who had very nearly caused her to plunge to the bindii-covered ground below.

It was the boy again, the one who had been drifting outside school earlier today talking to Alice, the same boy Gus had seen at the drive-in the day after they'd first arrived.

Up close, she saw the boy had freckles to match his short ginger hair, as well as stick-thin arms and legs poking out of his checked shirt and rolled-up jeans.

'Better watch your step there. You almost fell,' the boy observed. His green eyes were smiling as he said this.

'I was fine until you distracted me,' Gus pointed out.

'If you say so,' the boy replied.

'I *do* say so,' Gus said.

'Well, don't let me put you off,' the boy said.

'Fine. I won't,' Gus replied between gritted teeth.

She went back to scrubbing the bat poo off the drive-in screen. She was self-conscious now though with an audience and her technique was ineffectual. The purple smear was stubborn and hard to remove.

Out of the corner of her eye she saw the boy standing in the shade of the metal poles supporting the screen, squinting in the afternoon sun.

'You're doing it wrong,' he said after a while.

'Oh,' said Gus, dropping the broom in the bucket. 'Well, in that case—' She climbed down the ladder and handed him the broom and bucket. He looked taken aback. He didn't accept them right away.

'Since you're the expert apparently, you can have a go,' Gus instructed. 'I have more important things to do anyway. In the projection room.'

'I take it you're the new projectionist,' the boy said.

'That's right,' Gus said warily. 'How did you know that?'

'Your sister told me.'

Gus remembered seeing him and Alice speaking at the school fence. 'Oh,' she replied. 'Who are you, anyway?'

'I'm Stevie,' said the boy.

'I'm Gus,' she replied. 'My family are running this place for a while,' she said. 'Are you a maintenance person or something?'

She hadn't recalled Deirdre saying anything about that when they'd first arrived. Stevie shook his head. She set the bucket and broom down. 'Then what are you doing here?'

'I suppose I'm just a movie fan,' he said.

This boy didn't give much away, Gus thought. When he spoke it was slowly, annoyingly so.

'I saw you at school,' Gus continued, trying to draw him out.

'Yeah, I'm around,' Stevie said.

'Do you live near here?' Gus pressed. There weren't any houses around the drive-in.

The boy paused. 'I'm really just staying in Calvary temporarily,' he said.

Gus looked at him for further explanation.

'I'm — I'm waiting to be picked up,' he said. 'If you must know, I'm waiting for my mum to get me.'

Gus wanted to ask a million more questions, but something on his face told her not to pry deeper. 'Well,' she said, 'I really do have to do some work in the projection room.'

'Fine,' said Stevie mildly. 'Go. But tell me, what are you going to show?'

'Um,' said Gus.

'Which movie have you picked?' Stevie prompted. 'For the re-opening on Friday?'

This person asks a lot of questions, Gus thought. How did he know about the re-opening anyway? Alice, she supposed.

'It better be a good one,' Stevie continued. 'Mr Cronk has set the bar high.'

'I don't exactly know yet,' Gus said, trying not to sound panicked.

Stevie whistled long and low through his teeth. 'You should get a wriggle on. The movie is always published in the local paper on Fridays. Isn't the newspaper deadline tomorrow?'

'Why does everyone keep saying that?' Gus moaned.

She sat on the ground below the screen. She needed to think. She needed to act fast. She wished they had the internet here so she could search for movies online. Maybe she could borrow her mum's phone?

Stevie sat down beside her. 'As someone who has seen a lot of movies at the Starlight, I can tell you with certainty that people will look at what you're screening with their morning cereal. If you want customers, you have to advertise. And you have to pick a killer movie.'

She put her head in her hands and let out a moan. Who was she kidding? She was out of her depth.

'You need help,' Stevie observed.

'Yes!' Gus wailed.

'Well, I suppose *I* could help you,' Stevie said. 'My knowledge of genres and movies is encyclopaedic.'

'OK,' said Gus, wary but desperate. 'I need all the help I can get.'

'All right then,' Stevie mused. 'What have you seen in Mr Cronk's collection that appeals to you? We can start there.'

'I don't know,' Gus said panicked. 'I haven't heard of any of those old movies in the tins.'

'Wait, what? Where have you been? Under a rock?' Stevie asked incredulously.

'The city, I guess,' Gus replied, shrugging.

'Well, you've been missing out, Gus Able. I was raised on the classics. Everything I've learned about friendship, betrayal and flying sidekicks I've learned from movies pre-dating the twenty-first century. And I've learned it all sitting on the roof of a station wagon at the Starlight.'

'Really? The roof?' Gus repeated.

'You have a lot to learn, my friend,' Stevie informed her.

Gus didn't react to the f-word. 'So it would appear,' she said.

'So, back to the movie you're going to choose,' Stevie continued. 'I am a big believer in following your instincts with these kinds of things. If you feel good about your choices, others will too. They'll flock to your good taste and buy synthetic-flavoured popcorn by the bucketload.'

'It sounds great,' said Gus, 'but how do I choose a movie like that?'

'Think about the type of stories you like,' Stevie suggested. 'What do they have in them?'

'Um,' said Gus. 'Adventure, maybe?'

'Great, adventure, we can work with that. And what else do they have?'

'Um, fantasy, I guess? And a magical fictional universe.'

'OK, great, we can work with that too. What else?'

'I like it when there's mistaken identity,' Gus said, warming to her theme. 'Oh, and when the heroine saves herself!'

'Mistaken identity,' Stevie mused. 'Heroine saves herself ...'

Gus held her breath.

Stevie looked skywards, concentrating. 'I've got it,' he said after a moment. He smiled broadly. 'You're going to screen *The Princess Bride*.'

'I don't know about the title,' said Gus doubtfully. 'It sounds kind of ... girly.'

'Trust me,' Stevie said. 'I know the Starlight crowd.'

'If you say so,' she replied, still dubious. 'I think I saw that somewhere on the shelf ...'

Gus knew she had no choice but to trust him.

'You can thank me later,' Stevie informed her.

'We'll see after the box office is counted, I guess.' She found herself smiling though.

'Now, go place that ad,' Stevie said.

'Thanks, Stevie,' said Gus. 'So I suppose I'll see you around?'

'Sure, I guess,' Stevie said. 'I have time.'

Chapter 11

Too quickly it was Friday. A week had passed and the grand re-opening of the Starlight Drive-In Movie Theatre (and drycleaners) was upon them.

At dusk, the Able family gathered under the awning of the Moonbeam Cafe. They all sat at one of the scuffed aluminium picnic tables to share a meal of chicken nuggets and tinned corn. Fruit bats screeched in the mango trees, causing Gus and her siblings to jump mid-dinner.

Their mother was assigning the children jobs and behaving in a way Gus had never seen before. She seemed, well, organised. She had chosen three dishes from Deirdre's recipe collection to prepare and practised all week. She had written the menu with flourishes on a chalkboard she had found in the cafe storeroom. Mrs Able seemed nervous, as though she really cared about whether this evening was a success or not.

Her curly hair was pinned up and she wore a pretty sundress as well as the gold sandals she saved for special occasions. She swallowed the last bite of her dinner and dusted crumbs from her hands.

'Right,' Mrs Able began. 'Alice, have you got the float ready? Deirdre said people pay in cash around here.'

'Yes, Mum, I told you it's counted and ready to go, remember?'

'Great. And the tickets?' her mother enquired.

'I've got two rolls loaded and ready to dispense,' confirmed Alice.

'Well done, darling.'

Their mother turned to Artie. 'Mate, have you filled the sauce bottles and the serviette dispensers?'

'Yes, Mum,' he replied. 'And I stocked the drinks fridge, like you asked.'

'Good work, Artie,' their mother said, ruffling his hair.

She turned to her middle child. Mrs Able's expression set off butterflies in Gus's stomach — they misted above her solar plexus like a rainstorm. She could see in her mother's eyes how much this fresh start meant.

'How about you, Gus?' her mother asked.

Her look said, *Please don't disappoint me.*

Gus nodded. 'I think it's all under control, Mum. I placed the ad in *The Calvary Post*. I've warmed up the projector. And I'm about to load the film.'

Her mother's face broke open in a smile. 'Great, Gus. Well, I guess this it. Places, everyone,' Mrs Able said.

The kids scattered. Alice went serenely down the drive towards the ticket booth, her long hair swishing behind her, while Artie ran to switch on the drive-in lights. Her mother donned an apron and stood behind the counter, serving spoon in hand. Gus headed up the stairs to the projection room atop the cafe.

She pushed open the blue door, which made a shushing sound over the tatty carpet. At least the worst of the dust was gone due to her cleaning efforts. She had vacuumed and dusted the whole afternoon after school and even polished the projection room windows until they gleamed. Gus flicked on the light, walked to the machine and patted the projector gingerly. It whirred gently under her hands.

haunted and no one would turn up. She sincerely hoped Nicole was wrong.

'I placed the ad in the paper like you said,' she replied.

Gus fiddled with the reel. She couldn't seem to get the take-up spool to accept the film.

'You're doing it wrong,' Henry said then.

'What?' replied Gus anxiously. 'How?'

'The spool guide only accepts the film the right way. It's sensitive like that. It's so you don't show the movie upside down or back to front.'

'Oh,' said Gus.

'Want me to talk you through it again?'

Gus nodded and Henry instructed her to hold the reel carefully up to the light to examine the titles. He looked at Gus, surprised when he saw the name of the movie.

'*The Princess Bride*,' he said. 'Good choice.'

'It was recommended by a—'

Gus stopped herself. She almost said by *a friend*. But Gus didn't do friends.

'It was recommended by someone,' she corrected herself.

Henry instructed her about the right way to load the film. 'Make sure the audio side of the tape is facing you. That's the thicker side. The laser needs to read it so we have sound. That's right,' he said, watching her thread the film through all the various loops, cogs and reels. 'Tape it to the bottom reel so it doesn't fly off.'

Gus did as instructed and her stomach butterflies were reduced to a dull roar.

'All that's left to do is flick the motor switch and open the shutter. Then we'll be off and racing,' Henry said.

She felt better already, like the evening was in good hands. She had no idea how she would have done all that without Henry's guidance.

Gus opened the ancient curtains covering the projection room window and the last of the afternoon light streamed through the window.

Gus liked the feeling of being up high in the projection room, surveying the drive-in. There weren't yet any cars parked up against the space-age-looking speakers. Gus hoped they would arrive in droves soon. She looked at the clock above the window. It was ten minutes to showtime. They were cutting it fine.

The Starlight Drive-In Movie Theatre (and drycleaners) sign flickered, presumably switched on by Artie somewhere on the ground below. As the bulbs lit up the dusky sky, Gus felt the butterflies start up again, batting against her insides. Were they playing football in there?

She looked through the window to the ticket booth at the entrance, where Alice sat, reading a maths textbook while she waited to be inundated by moviegoers. From her vantage point, Gus saw her mother leaning against the side wall of the cafe, peering into the sunset towards town, as though willing carloads of patrons to appear.

'Where are they all?' she asked, turning to look at Henry.

The man in the terry-towelling hat shook his head. 'Dunno, Gus. Getting the punters in can be tricky lately. Maybe it was the choice of film.'

Gus's heart sank to her shoes.

Then she heard the sound of wheels crunching up the gravel drive. She turned back to the window, elated, but her heart sank again when she saw it was a police car. The officer driving the vehicle stopped at the ticket booth and spoke to Alice. They exchanged cash and tickets and he drove off slowly. Her sister's large eyes watched him down the drive.

Gus held her breath as she watched the police car pull up outside the cafe. A tall sandy-haired man got out and strode towards her mother. It wasn't the first time the police had come to ask Mrs Able questions. Gus swallowed as she thought of the sky-blue car parked by the caravan, Troy's car. She recalled the library book she hadn't returned. Both were stolen property. Had the officer come to arrest them? She crept down the projection room steps to eavesdrop, her heart thrashing in her chest.

Rather than pull out his notebook, however, the man produced his movie tickets, perused the menu board and began to place an order for dinner.

'I'll have the fisherman's catch and a lasagne topper,' the man said to Mrs Able. 'And a strawberry milkshake and diet lemonade, please.'

Her mother nodded and wrote the order down. It seemed a lot of food for one person.

'I'm Sergeant Terry Peters, by the way.'

Her mother smiled but did not offer her own name. 'Take a spot,' she said, 'and my son will bring the food over when it's ready. You can have first pick.'

Sergeant Peters smiled back, adjusted his glasses and ambled back to his car. Instead of climbing into the driver's seat, Sergeant Peters went around to the back right passenger seat and opened the door.

Gus held her breath. Was he going to escort a criminal to the drive-in? Or had he brought Troy, all the way from their old city, to identify them as thieves? Would they be watching *The Princess Bride* in handcuffs?

Instead of Troy, however, Sergeant Peters assisted an elderly woman out of the vehicle.

'Artie,' called their mother, who was watching from the kitchen. 'Can you help Sergeant Peters, please?'

Gus's little brother appeared and supported the elderly lady while the police officer produced a wheelchair from the boot of the car. Together they helped the woman into the chair and Artie wheeled the woman to her speaker of choice, while she gave him directions.

'Good choice, Mum,' Gus heard Sergeant Peters say.

Sergeant Peters produced a folding chair from the boot and set it down beside his mother. Relieved, Gus dashed back up the stairs to the projection room. It must be almost time to start the movie.

As she entered Henry spoke. 'Never in fifty years have I started a film late,' he said. 'And I don't intend to start today.'

Gus looked at the clock. It was seven pm on the dot.

'It's time to flip the motor switch and open the shutter, Gus,' Henry instructed.

Gus did as she was told. She heard coughing and then the blip of what sounded like a retro video game. Gus faced the big screen and saw the sound was coming not from Henry, but from the movie now being projected, one tiny frame at a time, onto the giant drive-in screen.

She gazed at the screen and saw the titles for *The Princess Bride* glide onto the great white page suspended in the sky. She felt her heart swell the way it did when she was reaching the end of a good book and it looked like everything would be OK for the main character.

'Go on,' said Henry, a friendly note under his gruff tone. 'It's best the first time you watch it.'

Gus dragged a dusty metal chair from the pile in the corner and placed it at the projection room window, just short of the light beam transporting the image onto the screen. She did as Henry instructed and watched the story unfold. The speakers on the projection room wall allowed them to hear the intro music and dialogue despite the whir of the movie projector.

She met the characters, farm boy Wesley, and the beautiful Buttercup, and absorbed the enchanting countryside, straight out of a fairy tale. She sat back in her chair and let the story take her over.

Feeling safe in the hands of the storytellers, she was only half-aware of Artie taking Mrs Peters and the police officer their order. Her brother sat beside the woman in the wheelchair and together they gasped and laughed, munched and cried, and cheered and booed at the screen. Alice joined them when she was satisfied there weren't any more patrons arriving at the ticket booth.

About half an hour in, another moviegoer did appear. A skinny figure slunk up the drive, and stood by the largest mango tree, gazing at the screen. From time to time, he mouthed lines of the film's dialogue and occasionally wielded an imaginary sword in the fight scenes alongside Wesley. Gus smiled at the back of Stevie's head. She had him to thank for this choice. It was a good one, she thought, even if the rest of the town weren't there to see it.

Midway through the film, the police officer headed to the cafe under the projection room and shortly returned to his seat with more food. Miraculously their customers were coming back for seconds. It sure was a smaller crowd than she had expected. Twenty per cent of two tickets was exactly four dollars profit, but the film had no less impact. Not even the shock of a fruit bat pooing mid-flight directly onto the screen during the climactic scene, when Wesley recovered from being 'mostly dead', could dampen the small but enthusiastic crowd's enjoyment.

'Well, what did you think?' Henry asked Gus as the final credits rolled.

'I'd call that a success,' she replied, her eyes shining.

'Would you now?' replied Henry.

'Yes,' said Gus. 'No one got food poisoning or asked for a refund. That's success in my book.'

'Low expectations, I see,' said Henry.

But he was smiling, too.

Chapter 12

Others had a different opinion about the success of the re-opening event.

On Saturday morning, before they were properly awake, Deirdre's big car rolled into the Starlight Drive-In Movie Theatre (and drycleaners), the tyres crunching gravel like corn flakes. The Director of the local Amateur Dramatic Society banged on the corrugated door of the caravan.

'Delphine!' she cried. 'Open *up*!'

Their mother stumbled to the door, tying a robe over her nightie and running a hand through her tangle of silvery-dark curls before opening the door.

'Delphine! What a *shame*,' Deirdre cried.

She was wearing a long black velvet dress with a lace ruffle even though it was already twenty-four degrees, and seven o'clock in the morning.

'Er, thanks,' said their mother. 'Why is that, exactly?'

'*Why*? The Friday night *turnout*, of course! *Very* disappointing, Delphine.'

'Oh,' said their mother, 'that.' Mrs Able's shoulders sagged.

'You'll need to do better than *two* patrons to keep the Starlight alive, my *dear*.'

'Yes, Miss Cronk. Though, there is the matter of the rumours—'

'I've heard from my solicitor,' Deirdre interrupted, 'and it's looking *good* for my application to fast-track the er, *deceased estate*. A matter of weeks, perhaps. In the meantime, I need the Starlight to pay its way. We agreed on the terms, Delphine.'

'So, you're planning on selling the Starlight soon, Miss Cronk?'

'That's none of your business, Delphine.'

Their mother bit her lip. 'Of course.'

The Director of the Amateur Dramatic Society continued, oblivious to Mrs Able's despair. 'As your *employer*, I need to stress, selling tickets is *paramount*. How *else* am I going to fund my *theatre* production?'

'Oh, I see,' said Mrs Able.

Chapter 13

A few days later, as she ate afternoon tea, Gus sat on the bottom step of the stairs to the projection room and brooded, even worse than a star in a romantic comedy. While they'd built on their audience over the weekend with four locals attending the Saturday screening of *The Princess Bride* and seven on Sunday night, it was very clear they hadn't yet covered costs.

She had declined her mother's offer of leftover delights from the Moonbeam Cafe and instead ate the first of the mulberries to fruit on the straggly tree by the drive-in boundary. The berries stained her fingers a deep red and she saw fruit was strewn all over the ground. She scuffed at one with her thong. We're becoming just like the locals, Gus thought, adopting their attire and diet, if not entirely being embraced by the residents of Calvary in return.

She was mad at Deirdre for not mentioning a few key details earlier in the agreement.

While the Director of the Amateur Dramatic Society had alluded to her father's death on appointing them the new caretakers of the Starlight, she had neglected to mention that he had thereupon turned into a ghost. Understandably, and as Nicole had pointed out at school, this was off-putting to moviegoers for a number of reasons, not the least being having your popcorn stolen.

How were they supposed to raise the drive-in from its sickbed now?

And if they did fail, where would they go then?

Calvary wasn't so bad, she supposed, if you didn't mind the bats and the food at the Moonbeam. Not to mention the patchy internet. As far as Gus could tell, Troy hadn't followed them there. While a police officer had shown up at the drive-in on Friday, bringing on that self-imploding feeling, he had merely been after a strawberry milkshake and fisherman's catch from the cafe, whatever that was. He appeared to have no interest in their mother's employment history as a spiritual medium at all. Or her supposed debts.

That was something they had to keep concealed if they wanted to stay. As far as Gus was concerned, her mother could keep cooking yellow foods and serving them up to the townspeople if that's what they wanted. It was the perfect cover for their shadowy past.

Although in order to stay, they had to get more patrons to the drive-in and Deirdre's visit had confirmed this.

But how? Gus mused. According to Stevie this came down to the movies selected. He had been right about the last movie. Though the audience had been small, it had been effective. *The Princess Bride* had made even her mother tear up, Mrs Able had reported. She told Gus she had been dabbing at her eyes with a serviette while washing up at the Moonbeam kitchen sink.

From her seat on the steps, Gus looked up at the great white screen for inspiration, or at least for Stevie. Today there was no sign of him.

She sighed. She needed the program solved. It was already Wednesday and she was due to place the ad in the newspaper today for this weekend's screening. They needed to build on word of mouth from the weekend. She would have to select a film all on her own.

She rose and walked up the steps to the projection room.

As always, the blue door protested on opening. As Gus entered, dust motes danced in a slice of light coursing through the window, as though they had been displaced by someone moving about the room. She heard the low hum of a tune being whistled. Someone was rifling in the reel cupboard.

The hairs on her neck fizzled. Was the ghost of Henry Cronk here again?

'Henry?' she called, moving into the room. 'Are you in there?'

Calm down, she told her thumping heart. Henry's not a *scary* ghost. A bit grumpy maybe, but helpful in his way, which was as mysterious to her as Mrs Able's psychic abilities.

'Henry?' she tried again.

There was a bang.

She took refuge behind the projector.

'Is that you, Gus?'

It was him all right. From there she could see a generous behind in a familiar pair of worn work shorts. The rest of Henry was in the cupboard peering at the movie canisters. What was he doing there in the daytime?

'Yes, it's me,' she croaked.

'Thank goodness. For a moment I thought it might be Deirdre.'

He emerged and moved towards where she stood. 'I've been waiting for you to arrive.'

His tone was less sinister than his words.

'Um, really?' Gus replied. 'What are you doing in here?'

'I suppose you could say I'm having a little stocktake. Getting things in order. Deirdre was always at me to do it.'

'Oh,' said Gus.

'Lend me your eyes, would you?'

Gus took a step back. Her heart was racing as fast as a length of film through the projector.

'Um ...' she replied.

'You seem a bit nervy today,' Henry remarked. 'I just need your help to read something. My eyes aren't what they used to be.' He pointed at a canister on the table. 'Can you tell me what this label says?'

Gus strained to read the faded penmanship on the tape. 'I think it says *Back to the Future*?' she guessed.

'Right. Good. Write that one down under Comedy. Or should it be Fantasy?'

'I'm not sure ...' Gus admitted.

'You're right. Put it in under both categories,' Henry instructed.

'OK,' said Gus. 'But um, Henry?'

'No need to take all day about it. We've got a lot of sorting to do.'

'But where should I write it?'

'Do I have to spell out everything?' Henry sighed. 'Write it in my manual, of course. It's on the shelf over there. We're categorising films by genre and era today.'

Gus retrieved a large leather-bound book from the shelf where Henry indicated. 'Is this it?'

'Yes,' the ghost confirmed. 'Now hop to it. I'm not getting any younger.'

'Yes, Mr Cronk,' Gus replied.

Deirdre had mentioned her father's manual when they'd first arrived, Gus recalled. She had expected it to be a booklet with diagrams of the parts of the Kalee projector and instructions for how it worked. Henry's manual was so much more. The leather-bound book was stuffed with movie posters and receipts and articles clipped from the local newspaper. Gus saw a news report about somebody's pet crocodile escaping and another about how the price of eggs had gone up scandalously.

There were photos too — a picture of a much younger Henry and a woman in a red dress with dark curly hair, as well as a man in riding clothes and an Akubra hat. The three stood arm in arm in front of the Starlight screen, smiling. Behind them, a film title loomed large: *The Man from Snowy River*. Were they movie stars? Gus wondered. Maybe the Starlight really had been something all those years back.

Gus flicked through the pages of the manual and saw lists and lists of movies written down in Henry's neat cursive. Under each was a short review and the date it was screened at the drive-in. This was more than an instruction manual. It was a history book, the history of the Starlight.

'What does this one say?' Henry asked, interrupting Gus's reading.

Gus peered at the label on the tin Henry was pointing to. 'I think it says *Labyrinth*?' she replied. 'Sounds like it should be under Fantasy?'

'Spot on, Gus. You're not half bad at this. You've certainly surpassed my expectations.'

Gus smiled and decided not to take offence. She was surprised to find she was enjoying herself, despite being in the presence of a ghost.

Henry seemed so excited today, like a younger version of himself. He seemed so … alive. It was hard to believe he, well, wasn't. Still, everyone said he had passed over. That's why they were staying away, apparently, to the Able family's detriment.

But does it have to be? Gus thought suddenly. Maybe, she told herself, they could work *with* the situation instead of against it. It was something she heard her Gran tell their mother to try, when they'd stayed at the farm that time.

'Hey, Henry,' she said slowly, thinking aloud. 'You don't know of any *ghost* movies, do you? I think I'm in the mood for something spooky.'

'*Ghost* movies?' repeated Henry. 'You've moved on from fantasy films now? That's quite a leap, Gus. Kids these days,' he added, shaking his head. He considered the shelves containing boxes and boxes of film. 'Supernatural isn't really my genre. But I'm sure I have something in our collection,' he mused.

He turned back to the cupboard and peered at the canisters on the next to bottom shelf. 'Aha,' he said, his voice muffled by the metal. 'What about *The Fog*? Or *Poltergeist*?'

'They sound a bit spooky,' Gus said. Maybe too much so. 'I guess I was thinking of something that was more family friendly.'

'A *family* ghost movie?' Henry replied sceptically.

'Yeah,' said Gus. 'That way we can sell more tickets.'

'I like the way your mind works, Gus,' said Henry, disappearing into the cupboard again. 'Hmm, let me see …'

Gus too began to rifle through the cupboard until her hand lit upon a canister in the carton named Comedy. She retrieved it and held it out to Henry.

'What about this?' she suggested.

Henry read the title aloud. '*Ghostbusters*?' he replied. 'Huh. This was a major hit in 1984. I'm referring to the original film, of course.' He paused. 'You know, I think that might just work.'

Gus smiled. 'Great,' she said, setting the film down. 'I'll let the newspaper know *Ghostbusters* will be screening all weekend.'

'You run along now. Got to give the punters plenty of notice.'

'OK,' agreed Gus. 'And thanks for your help, Henry,' she said.

Before she could escape and call the newspaper, Gus heard the crunch of tyres on gravel. She peered out the projection room window, expecting to see the big maroon sedan. It wasn't Deirdre's car, however but a smaller one, red and zippy looking. *Calvary Realty* was printed in enthusiastic font on the side of the car.

When Gus turned around to ask if Henry was expecting anyone — a silly question, she realised a second later, given he was made of memories and vapour — the man was gone.

Where did he go? she wondered. Did he sleep in the movie reel cupboard like some kind of film-buff vampire?

She was distracted by voices outside. She moved to the window to see what was going on. The occupants of the car had got out and were walking around the drive-in, kicking at the gravel and banging on the radio posts with their knuckles. They appeared to be inspecting the place.

Gus recognised the woman by her dress sense. It was Deirdre, this time in a purple satin number, fresh from rehearsals presumably. She was with a man in a blue suit who had large white teeth and another man in a brown suit with oiled-down hair. The blue suit snapped photographs as Deirdre gave them a tour. Brown suit was taking notes.

'Fantastic square metreage. Did you know it is zoned light industrial out here? Huge potential for the site after it's cleared,' the blue-suited man enthused.

'Cleared? So, you don't think the *buildings* are worth anything, Mr Carmichael?' Deirdre enquired. 'Nor the *equipment*?'

'Not in this digital age,' Mr Carmichael said.

'Not even as a curiosity or *museum* piece?' Deirdre pressed.

'People stream now, Deirdre. It's the land that's worth a bomb,' the man replied. 'Situated right by the highway like this, the parcel would be perfect for an industrial site, or a new housing estate.'

He took a photo of the caravan and the line of mango trees. Gus bristled. Why was he taking pictures of their home?

'I suppose you would be the *expert*, Mr Carmichael, although, dear old *Dad* would be disappointed to have his precious drive-in destroyed,' Deirdre said. 'However I am happy to hear the *site* is worth *something*.'

Before she realised what she was doing, Gus leaned out the window. 'Can I help you?' she called.

'Oh *halloo*,' Deirdre called, looking startled. 'No, we're fine, dear. I'm just showing Mr Carmichael and Mr Mayne *around*.'

Mr Mayne, the man in the brown suit, grunted in acknowledgment and wrote something in his notebook.

'You do realise we're closed today,' Gus said.

'Not to worry, *dear*, they just wanted to *see* the place. For ... *insurance* purposes. I'm the owner-to-*be*, after all,' she said sweetly.

Mr Carmichael was now pacing the perimeter, stepping it out as though counting the metreage. He jogged back to Deirdre looking as though he might bust out of his suit from excitement.

'I think we've got something here,' the man said to Mr Mayne on his return. 'If Miss Cronk has the buildings dozed and installs fibre optic cabling, it'll be a real return on investment, as we say in my game.'

Mr Mayne's eyebrows twitched. He turned to Deirdre. 'What do you think, Deirdre?'

'You mean *sell* the property to *developers*? I *did* have *plans* for the land *myself*. Perhaps as an *artistic* and *cultural* centre of *excellence*. The latest *commedia dell'arte*, the local pet portrait *show*, you know, a *hub*. It's been a little *dream* of mine for some *time*. I'm not *saying* I would call it the Deirdre Cronk Centre of Artistic Excellence or *anything*, but something along those *lines* might do ...'

'That does sound lovely,' Mr Mayne agreed. 'But Deirdre, how do I put this? Mr Carmichael thinks you are sitting on valuable real estate.'

'There's going to be a lot of interest if we go to market,' Mr Carmichael said, smiling broadly. His forehead was shining.

'How *much* interest?' Deirdre asked shrewdly.

Mr Mayne wrote something in his notebook and handed it to Deirdre. 'I bet my gold watch we get that many zeros,' he informed her.

Deirdre's jaw dropped. Mr Carmichael looked at the figure on the page and nodded, indicating he agreed.

'You're confident we'll get *that* much?' Deirdre asked Mr Carmichael, recovering.

He nodded.

'What's your *commission*, sir?' Deirdre practically shouted.

'Three point seven per cent. It's a little on the high side, but I'm told I'm worth it,' Mr Carmichael said smoothly.

Mr Mayne cleared his throat. 'As your legal counsel, I'd advise you to sign Calvary Realty as your agency,' he said.

It took less than a second for Deirdre to stick out her hand. Not so long ago she had shaken hands with Gus's mother, which had been for a completely different deal.

'*Done*,' she said to Carmichael. 'You've got the *job*, sir.'

All three beamed, but Gus was fuming. She felt her hands clench into fists at her sides.

She'd got the gist of what was happening. Blue suit was a real estate agent and brown suit was some kind of lawyer probably. So Deirdre *was* planning to sell this place. Is that why Deirdre told her mother their arrangement as caretakers was temporary? And what about her dear departed father's wishes, that they continue to screen movies?

'It's almost a shame to let it go,' the agent continued looking around. 'And I never say that. This place is just so quaint.'

Gus had heard enough. 'I said, we're closed,' she told them through gritted teeth.

'Just finishing up, dear,' said Deirdre.

Her voice was light, but Gus could tell the Director of the Amateur Dramatic Society's teeth were gritted too.

'Come back Friday,' she told them. 'Seven pm sharp. We're screening *Ghostbusters*. The original.'

'My *word*,' tittered Deirdre. 'That will have them lining up down the *street*.'

She laughed and so did Mr Carmichael, his white teeth gleaming. Mr Mayne smiled thinly. Gus didn't like either of them.

She watched the three climb back in the zippy red car. They reversed and headed back into town. Gus felt her fists unclench at her side.

'Can you believe that?' Gus said to Henry when Deirdre and the two suits were out of sight.

But Henry was gone, she remembered. He'd slipped out before.

Gus didn't blame him for not wanting to see Deirdre, after their disagreement before he'd died.

She was beginning to see why he hadn't got on with his daughter.

She banged the window shut and went downstairs to call the newspaper before they closed. Tonight it was her turn to help their mother with dinner. They would need something to accompany the movie theme on the menu, she mused. Maybe if they could get a good crowd, Deirdre might change her mind about selling.

Chapter 14

'Hello, you must be Augusta.'

A woman wearing a rainbow tie-dyed dress opened the front door and welcomed Gus inside. 'I'm Peta Chagall, Nicolette's primary caregiver.'

Gus looked at the woman, confused. She had navigated a jungle of wind chimes in the yard to arrive at a pink front door decorated with fairies, butterflies and hand-painted toadstools. It was like an obstacle course, Gus thought. A tinkly, musical obstacle course.

'Do I have the right house?' Gus asked. 'I'm looking for Nicole.'

'You've come to the right place. I'm Nicole's mother,' the woman explained. 'Although I prefer the non-gendered term "caregiver".'

'Oh,' said Gus. 'Is Nicole home?'

Nicole's mother nodded. She wore her hair shaved on the left side while long brown curls cascaded on the right. She had a tattoo of the sun on her neck and another of a dolphin swimming up her arm. Something told Gus that Nicole's mother and Mrs Able would like each other.

'Yes, she's just clearing stagnant chi in her room.'

Gus blinked.

'Anyway, do come in,' the caregiver said. 'I am just making you girls a green smoothie. Nicole told me about your dietary … openness, so I've added extra apple today.'

She gave Gus an encouraging smile as they stood in the living room. She seemed nervous somehow. Gus felt nervous too. While seeing a ghost was disconcerting, so was going to a classmate's house. But she forced her mouth into a smile. Her eyes lit on a stack of dream catchers, piled on the wooden coffee table. They were made from sticks and a blend of riotous wools and adorned with feathers and beads. The dream catchers had price tags looped through their weaves.

'I make them,' Peta Chagall informed her, following Gus's gaze. 'I sell them at the Sunday markets in town. They're for protection. I can make you one, if you like.'

Gus was pretty sure she'd need something stronger to shift Henry's presence from her life. 'Um, thank you. But I'm OK for the moment,' she said.

The woman studied her but called out, 'Nicolette! Augusta is here.'

There was no reply.

'She's been waiting for you,' Ms Chagall informed Gus. She looked at Gus and smiled widely before saying, 'I'll go get the snacks.'

Nicole's mother headed to the kitchen. Left alone in the living area, Gus looked around.

Nicole's lounge room was like the inside of a crystal shop, with pink quartz and third eyes strung up everywhere. The books on the shelves included titles like: *The Rainbow Chakra Light* and *The Inner Witch: How to tap into your white magic powers*.

Nicole rushed into the living room and then slowed her pace, as though she hadn't been waiting for Gus at all. 'Oh hi,' she said casually. 'Ready to get started? My room is this way.'

Gus followed her science partner down the hall.

Unlike the rest of the house, Nicole's room was quite sparse. The furniture was simple, and the bedcover was white and plain. There wasn't a third eye or dream catcher to be found. There was a small silver laptop on the wooden desk, however, displaying a webpage featuring a giant pulsing comet. The image accompanied an online news article by *The Calvary Post*, the same newspaper she advertised their movies in. The headline screamed in red font: *Is Riley's Comet the harbinger of doom?* The tagline read: *How to prepare for a comet apocalypse.*

Wow, thought Gus, the locals were really concerned about this comet.

Nicole's maths and science certificates were displayed neatly above her desk but, apart from these adornments, the room lacked decoration. There weren't any old toys or birthday cards, clothes on the floor, or photos with friends pinned up. Nicole's room made Gus feel sad.

Nicole didn't ask Gus to sit down, so she perched on the desk awkwardly, beside the laptop. For a moment, she thought maybe she had been wrong about Nicole wanting to be friends. For some reason this made her feel even more glum. Gus told herself it was ridiculous she cared, given her own stance on friendship.

But then Nicole's face broke open like sunshine through a cloud. She grabbed her laptop and indicated

Gus should sit on her bed. Like a puppy, she couldn't contain her enthusiasm. When Nicole spoke next it was without pause, like a freight train.

'So, I've been thinking we need to wow Ms McKenzie with our comet assignment,' she said. 'We have to come up with something really cool and unexpected. It's got to be cutting edge. As well as, you know, factually accurate. Don't you agree? Everyone else is going to be doing a garbage bag around a Styrofoam ball and adding in some tinsel or something. I mean, how predictable. Boring! We need to think big,' she said, taking a breath. 'So, what have you got for me, Gus?'

Before Gus could reply, Nicole's mother entered bearing a bamboo tray. She handed each of them a tall glass of juice resembling pond water and a plate of snacks to share.

'Would you like a bliss ball?' Nicole's mum enquired, offering Gus the plate.

To Gus, the treats resembled the wallaby poos she had seen under the mango trees by the drive-in.

'Mum, please don't hover,' implored Nicole. 'We've got serious work to do here.'

'Of course, darling. But remember, only one hour of screen time, OK? We don't want to harm your developing brains with excess levels of electromagnetic radiation, do we?'

'Muh-um,' said Nicole.

'Nicole, you know very well the family values around field exposure theory. One hour on that thing tops, or your computer will go the way of the microwave.'

Peta Chagall mimed tossing a medium-sized appliance out the window. Gus's eyes widened.

'Fine,' huffed Nicole.

'Enjoy your snacks,' her mother sang.

She left the plate of bliss balls on Nicole's desk. The caregiver winked at Gus before she closed the door.

'Don't mind my mum. She's going to save the world from radiation sources *and* nutritional misdemeanours, one bliss ball at a time.'

'Haha,' replied Gus. She had to get something off her chest. 'Nicole,' she ventured. 'Doesn't it bother you?'

'Does what bother me?' asked Nicole.

Gus hesitated. 'What they call you at school. What the footy boys say.'

'What do they call me?' Nicole asked.

'You know, "Kale Girl" and things like that,' said Gus reluctantly. 'And they hurt you, Nicole. They shouldn't do that. We shouldn't let them.'

Gus surprised herself with the 'we'.

Nicole thought. 'I suppose it bothers me a little. But it's got to be someone, you know? And in our year, it happens to be me.'

This made Gus feel like she wanted to cry all of a sudden. She took a sip of her green juice and nearly spat it out again all over Nicole's bedspread. It tasted like something scraped up from the bottom of a chook yard.

'Besides, lately it's helped me to see how you handle it,' Nicole said brightly.

Gus's stomach gurgled. 'Um, handle what, Nicole?'

'You know, what those boys with the borderline average-IQs in our year say about your family.'

'Um, what do those boys say about my family, Nicole?' Gus asked.

'Oh, you didn't —? Nothing, never mind,' replied Nicole sounding flustered.

Gus stared at Nicole, willing her to speak. She both did and did not want to hear what her science partner had overheard. Nicole looked like she might cry when she finally spoke.

'It's mostly about your sister, Gus. I wouldn't worry.'

'Nicole, what do they say about Alice at school? Tell me.'

'Oh, just the usual stuff,' Nicole said hurriedly.

'Like what?' Gus prompted.

Nicole hesitated. 'Like that she's different. And not in a good way. That she's ... weird. Just things like that.'

'Weird?' Gus echoed, blood in her ears.

She recalled Alice laughing on the bench with a group of kids on their first day of school. And then Alice talking to Stevie after school and the look the kids kicking the soccer ball had exchanged about her.

'They think she's weird?' she repeated.

Nicole nodded. Her cheeks were red. 'I guess,' she said.

Gus absorbed this. She felt a bit sick. She was ninety-five per cent sure it wasn't due to the green juice.

'Anyway, don't worry about them, or what those boys say,' Nicole said. 'They are going to be teen fathers in footy shorts, who will work at Calvary Discount Auto Parts until they're as old as that comet. We, on the other hand,' continued Nicole, 'are going to be regular Nancy Grace Romans.'

Gus smiled, despite herself. 'Um, who?'

'You don't know who Nancy Grace Roman is? You seriously need to get to the library more.'

Gus couldn't help but agree. Nicole seized the laptop from her desk and typed something into Google. She clicked on a result and turned the laptop to face Gus. On the screen was a woman with her hair set in curls, wearing tortoiseshell glasses, standing beside a giant star-gazing contraption.

'Nancy Grace was only one of the most famous female astronomers of modern times. Like, she designed the Hubble telescope,' Nicole said incredulously.

'Oh, right,' said Gus, wiping her mouth. 'The Hubble.'

'We are in worse shape than I thought,' Nicole muttered. 'How are we going to ever win this thing?'

Gus appreciated the 'we' but had to confess she didn't know.

'Well, I thought you might say that,' Nicole said. 'So I've been doing some research. I think we should aim for our comet to be as realistic as possible. What did Ms McKenzie say a comet was made of again?'

'Um,' Gus said, digging deep into her memory for last week's lesson. 'Ice? Dust particles?' she guessed.

'Right!' confirmed Nicole, giving her a high-five. 'A comet is simply the frozen leftovers from when the solar system was made.'

'Wow,' replied Gus. 'I never thought of it that way.'

'So, here's what we're going to do,' Nicole instructed. 'We're going to demonstrate how the nucleus of a comet melts and turns to gas as it approaches the sun. I looked that up. This gives Riley's its halo and, as it travels across the sky, a distinctive tail. To demonstrate this properly, we'll need to work together, though.'

'OK,' said Gus.

'Here's my plan: you bring the dirt and gravel — you should have plenty at the drive-in — and I'll arrange the rest of the ingredients, including the chemicals and a heat source. When it's our turn to present in class, they'll be blown away!'

'Sounds cool,' Gus said.

Nicole's enthusiasm was infectious. Weirdly, for once, Gus felt excited about getting up in front of the class. Maybe they might even win. And planning the science assignment was a welcome change from thinking about her mum, or ghosts, or saving the drive-in, not to mention what Nicole had just said about Alice.

'What's the prize, again?' Gus asked.

'Don't you remember? A telescope for the town,' Nicole informed her. 'A proper one they can mount in a central spot to see the comet and … and other astronomical events.'

'Cool,' said Gus.

'But I'm not doing this for the Mega-scope,' Nicole confided, snapping the laptop closed. 'I'm doing it for the glory.'

Chapter 15

At six thirty pm on Friday night the Able family gathered around one of the Moonbeam's aluminium tables again, after a dinner of defrosted saveloy sausages in bread.

'All set, gang?' Mrs Able asked brightly. 'Lights, camera, action?'

She looked at her children in turn and they nodded.

'Can you believe we've got actual bookings for tonight?' she marvelled. 'I don't think that's happened for the last few years. I checked the records. It must be the movie you picked, Gus.'

She beamed at Gus and Gus smiled back. Rather than drain their mum, this job seemed to energise her. She actually seemed happy in the cafe, cooking the terrible food and talking to badly dressed locals. What had been a hideout had become a calling. She looked different too. She was wearing her gold sandals and her pretty dress at screenings, but that wasn't it. As Gus gazed at her mum she saw a light in her eyes she couldn't remember ever seeing before. She was glad.

From her spot at the table Gus could see into the kitchen where pots were simmering on the stove. As opposed to when they'd arrived, the Moonbeam looked very tidy and organised. The shelves and cabinets were stocked and surfaces were so clean they shined. Her mother had organised Deirdre's recipes into a series of labelled folders. Nothing like this had happened in any of the other places they'd stayed.

'I've been thinking,' continued Mrs Able. 'After we've covered the debts, we could get a computer. We could set up online bookings for the Starlight. You guys could use it for your homework too. What do you think?'

'Sounds awesome!' said Artie. 'We've never had our own computer before.'

'That would be cool,' Gus admitted.

Her mother had such grand plans. Gus was crossing her fingers behind her back in hope that the town would show up.

'In the meantime, Artie, I believe I owe you this,' Mrs Able said.

She produced a box wrapped in silver paper, which Artie promptly tore off.

'Optimus Prime!' he cried.

He ripped opened the packaging to free his prize and held it aloft.

'That's for your good work with the patrons,' their mother said.

'Thanks, Mum,' Artie said, holding the toy to his cheek.

'You're welcome. Let's go, Team Able!' said their mother. 'Now, places, everyone!'

Alice rolled her eyes but got up to go to the ticket booth.

'I'm going to wait for Mrs Peters by the gate,' said Artie. 'I told her last time I'd save her their spot.'

Together her brother and sister made their way down the drive, while their mother bustled into the kitchen.

At six forty-five pm Gus was pacing in the projection room.

Ghostbusters was loaded in the machine. This time Gus had fed the spools herself and got the projector working, under Henry's watchful eye, without the original projectionist for the Starlight saying a word.

'It feels hot,' she said patting the machine gingerly.

'It's working hard. You'll have to watch that,' Henry said. 'Overheating can be trouble. I've done my best with installing the fans and attending to good ventilation, but the set-up is getting pretty old now.'

He moved from his spot by the window. He'd been watching the patrons arrive. Sergeant Terry and his mother were already settled in their usual places. The police officer was shovelling in a second helping of dinner.

In addition to the usual menu items, Gus had googled the movie trailer and worked with her mother and siblings to create some desserts that tied in with the movie: green 'slime' jelly cups and marshmallows squished together to look like ghosts, with liquorice eyes. Sergeant Terry had selected one of each to follow his main course.

'If it's warm, we'll have to keep an eye on it,' Henry said.

His voice brought Gus back into the projection room.

She wondered what was going on in poor Henry the ghost's brain. And why was he hanging around anyway? She had overheard her mother telling Troy ghosts did that when they had unfinished business, when they needed the help of those still living. What does Henry need help with? Gus wondered.

Right now, however, Gus wasn't complaining. She had to admit she was grateful for Henry's assistance.

'Why is overheating trouble?' Gus wondered. 'Will the projector break down?'

'It could indeed, or worse. Film can be flammable,' Henry explained. 'It's covered in nitrate. At least, older-style film is. We don't want the movies to ignite or much less explode. Haven't you seen *Cinema Paradiso*?'

Gus shook her head.

'You are a disgrace to the profession of movie projection, Gus,' Henry said. 'But I think we're safe with *Ghostbusters*. They stopped using nitrate in the early nineteen fifties. We still better keep an eye on things. There are some pretty old classics in my collection. If they were to go up—'

Here Henry whistled.

She nodded to indicate she understood. Gus didn't want to jeopardise anything, especially now, when

148

people were actually queuing up at the Starlight ticket booth.

From the projection room window, Gus could see Alice selling tickets to a family in a white sedan, a bunch of kids hanging out the windows in a tangle of arms and legs. The limbs disappeared inside the car once their owners spotted Sergeant Peters and his police car. They were followed by an elderly couple in a pristine brown hatchback and then two cars full of teenagers, the drivers freshly licensed. That made nineteen people, Gus counted as each car selected a spot facing the screen. Artie helped them with their radio speakers. It looked like her film choice had been a good one. A movie that resonated with the punters, as Henry would say.

Meanwhile, Mrs Able was fussing in the kitchen, removing hot chips from the deep fryer and retying her apron before standing at the counter to take food orders as people began to queue at the Moonbeam. Several more cars were rolling up the drive and at six fifty-nine pm Gus counted thirty-two patrons, not including her family or Henry. It looked like they could make up for the previous slow weekend and maybe even be on their way towards making a profit.

The elderly couple had spread out a tartan rug in front of their car and were drinking tea from a Thermos.

It was by no means a full house, but Gus was happy. What was more, everyone appeared to be wearing covered footwear.

At seven pm sharp, she began rolling.

She half-expected to see Stevie rock up, to linger by the mango tree and scab a free ticket, but so far, he hadn't shown. Instead of watching the screen, Gus watched the moviegoers with delight as they took in the film.

About halfway through the movie, she needed a loo break. 'Can you keep an eye on things here, Henry? I'll be right back,' Gus said.

He nodded, engrossed in the story.

Gus picked her way through the crowd towards the toilet block.

She stopped to smile at Mrs Peters on the way; she sat in the same spot as last time. It made Gus happy to see they had repeat customers. Artie had again stationed himself beside her.

'Enjoying the movie, Mrs Peters?' she enquired.

'Oh yes,' said the woman. 'I do like a comedy.'

She reached for Gus's hand. 'But do you know what

I really like? A film with dancing,' she said, her eyes shining.

'Mrs Peters used to be the Calvary district ballroom dancing champion,' Artie piped up.

'Well, my husband and I were,' Mrs Peters said. 'And we were only semi-finalists,' she added modestly. 'It takes me back though to watch it on the big screen.'

Gus nodded. This sounded like their first movie request. 'I'll see what I can find for you,' she promised.

When Gus emerged from the loo she nearly collided with a patron. The toilet light had timed out and at that moment there was only a fingernail moon to see by. The person was a blur of flannelette without a face.

'Er, sorry,' Gus said, her heart in her teeth. 'You scared me!'

The person she had almost collided with began to laugh. 'Gus, is that you?' they asked.

She recognised his voice right away. It was Stevie, the drive-in freeloader. The screen went bright again and his string-bean form was illuminated.

'Stevie. What are you doing here?'

She had given up on seeing him tonight.

'Came to see how your programming was received,' he replied.

He looked over at the movie screen, the gauntness of his face highlighted by the shadows of the drive-in.

'Did you actually buy a ticket this time?' Gus enquired.

'Alice said it wasn't necessary,' Stevie responded, smiling.

'Did she?' Gus replied, making a face.

Maybe that was what they had been speaking about at school that day, when Gus had seen them together, talking over the fence — Stevie's freeloading — though she doubted it.

'Well, what do you think of the turnout?'

'Not too bad at all,' Stevie said, appraising the crowd. 'Ironic choice, given the rumours about this place.'

He smiled lopsidedly.

So Stevie knew about Henry too. It really was an open secret, just like Nicole had said.

One of the teenagers from school walked by, headed for the loos.

'You could have told me earlier about the ghost situation,' she whispered.

Stevie shrugged like it was no big deal.

He seemed distracted all of a sudden, scanning the crowd as though looking for someone. His gaze lit on

Alice, who was sitting on the grassy strip in front of the screen.

'I haven't seen you lately,' she said, trying to draw him back into the conversation. 'Where have you been?'

'Around,' Stevie said. 'What did I miss?'

'Um, only that Nicole in my class and I are hands down going to win the science competition.'

'Oh yeah?' he replied sceptically. 'What are you guys making?'

'The nucleus of a comet. We're using dirt and gravel, and … and, a bunch of highly flammable things,' she informed him.

'Sounds great. What could go wrong?' he replied.

They laughed.

'Actually, I know a little something about comets too,' Stevie said then.

'Oh yeah? What do you know exactly about tailed stars?' Gus demanded. 'See what I did there?'

'I know more than you might think,' he countered.

'I don't believe you.'

'Trust me, I have first-hand knowledge of space rock behaviour.'

'Prove it to me,' Gus said.

'Meet me behind the screen when the film is over and I'll show you,' he countered.

Gus's stomach flipped. She felt weird all of sudden, like she wasn't fully in her body.

Stevie smiled again. His teeth were very white in the dark, they glowed like bones. Gus smiled too, feeling reassured. If she hadn't had that strict policy about friends, Gus might have made an exception for Stevie. And maybe for Kale Girl too.

There was a loud crash and mood music thrummed through the speakers. Gus turned to watch, arrested for a moment by the movie. On the screen a man in coveralls had just been spattered in green slime. A cheeky green ghost was howling with laughter. The drive-in audience were all laughing too.

Gus turned back to Stevie, to tell him she would meet him later, but he was looking towards the crowd of moviegoers again. He was focused on one person in particular.

Stevie was gazing at Alice, who was watching the movie. Her sister's perfect face was reflected in the glow of the screen. Gus saw she looked different somehow from the Alice she had grown up with. Something about her had changed.

At that moment, the carful of boys from school appeared, roving through the crowd, apparently looking for kicks. When they saw Alice the kid in front began to point and laugh. The others joined in, jeering at Alice as they passed her sitting on the ground. Gus saw the ringleader was the boy called Nathan, the one who had targeted Nicole with the soccer ball.

Alice stayed still in her spot, her shoulders straight, but her serene expression slipped a little.

Gus exhaled shakily. She recalled what Nicole had said at her house about everyone at school thinking Alice was weird. Beside her, she could feel something rise off Stevie. Not heat exactly, or anger, but something palpable all the same.

'What's going on with Alice?' she asked aloud.

She looked at his eyes, which were large and dark and burning.

'Alice is different from other kids around here,' Stevie said. 'I reckon people have noticed.'

She hadn't expected him to answer, but what he said made sense. 'People always notice Alice,' Gus said.

It was true. But this time, maybe it was different, their noticing was not the good kind.

Stevie paused, as though considering whether to continue. They both looked up at the screen. 'Sometimes it frightens her. At least that's what she told me.'

Gus felt him staring at her now, and it made her feel strange.

'You're similar, you know,' Stevie told her. 'You and your sister.'

Gus didn't know what to say. Nobody had said she and Alice were similar before. 'I should get back to the projection room,' she said.

She turned to walk back up the stairs, then remembered what he had said about the comet. 'I'll meet you a bit later, like we agreed?' Gus called over her shoulder.

There was no reply.

When Gus turned back to confirm with Stevie, he had merged with the crowd.

Chapter 16

Gus wasn't sure if she had imagined their conversation during *Ghostbusters*, but there Stevie was after everyone had left, waiting by the blank screen.

She arrived around ten pm. After the final credits rolled, Gus had raced through the dishes piled in the Moonbeam sink and the nightly drive-in shutdown routine and then ducked off at bedtime on the pretext of brushing her teeth.

With the drive-in lights turned off, the stars showed up more in the night sky, glinting almost brashly, although Gus supposed they were always there, whether she noticed them or not. Stevie pointed to the exit under the sleeping drive-in sign. They were going off-site.

Are we heading to the library to research comets? Gus wondered. They would have to break in, like characters in a detective story. It probably wasn't a good idea. She already had a bad name at one library for not returning books.

Together they crunched up the gravel driveway of the Starlight, and continued on the road out of town, which was flanked by the silent canefields. They too were quiet as they walked. The only sound was the screech of a flying fox as it cursed the bare mango trees.

Gus trained the torch she had pinched from the caravan on the slick dark road as they walked. Stevie stopped when they reached a gap in the planted rows of cane.

'Let's go this way,' he said pointing to a dirt track. 'We'll follow the headland.'

'You mean, down there?' Gus asked.

She shone the torch on the track, at the end of which there appeared to be only darkness. The sugarcane rustled and danced to an invisible night tune. It made goosebumps rise on her skin.

'Yep,' said Stevie. 'You can trust me.'

'All right,' said Gus. 'But if you try to murder me, I'll come back and haunt you, I swear,' she warned.

'It's a deal,' Stevie replied.

He stepped onto the dirt track and Gus followed.

The cane formed an archway over the path as they walked, closing them off from the sky and stars. It seemed to Gus they were walking into the very heart of darkness. When she looked back towards the highway, the rows of cane appeared to have drawn closer, so that the entrance from the road was no longer visible. She told herself she had been reading too many spooky stories.

They had walked a few hundred metres when she heard the sound of water coursing steadily over stones.

In another twenty metres or so they were at a crossroad. Beyond the track, the bank sloped down to a wide river, just discernible through bordering gum trees.

'Coming?' Stevie asked.

Gus nodded and followed as he stepped over the headland. They picked their way down the bank to the water's edge.

They walked a way along the edge of the river through a twist of trees. After a while Stevie stopped. 'This is the spot,' he said.

Gus looked around, shining her torch into the night.

Paperbark trees dipped their roots into the dark water. Downriver a hundred metres or so, someone had built a crude fishing hut out of tin and fibro. There was a small deck extending out over the river with a chair and steel firepit. Gus let her eyes wander over the dark hut. It wasn't a bad set-up, considering. It seemed peaceful by the river.

This must have been where Henry had come to stay after his argument with Deirdre. He must have also disappeared somewhere around here, Gus thought. Deirdre had alluded to him vanishing by the river, the tragic fishing accident. Gus shivered, all of a sudden.

She spoke to distract herself from these thoughts.

'This place is cool, I guess. I don't understand what it has to do with the comet, though,' she said.

'Patience, my friend,' Stevie said. 'We have to dig a little to find it.' He crouched and gazed around the riverbank.

'Find what, exactly?' Gus replied.

'My space rock,' Stevie told her.

Her eyes widened. 'Are you saying there's a rock from outer space *here*?'

Stevie nodded. 'It's around this spot somewhere,' he confirmed, as though to himself. 'Near that pile of rocks I made. I know it.'

He peered at the bank and held his hands over the ground as though divining the location of the space rock through the mud. He meant they had to dig, literally, she realised.

Curious, Gus dropped to the ground too. She set the torch down and removed the larger of the rocks from the pile Stevie had indicated. She began to dig in the soft mud, and it wasn't long before her hands hit something hard, not far from the surface.

'Ow,' she said.

From the dirt she retrieved a piece of rock about the size of a chapter book, which was smooth and flat with tiny bubbles across the surface. Even in the dark Gus could tell it was an unusual colour and shinier than any river stone.

'Check it out,' Gus breathed, holding it out to him.

'Space rock,' Stevie confirmed.

'*Really?*' replied Gus.

'It's a meteorite,' Stevie clarified. 'A particle broken off from a meteor or comet or what have you, which survived the burn through the earth's atmosphere.'

'Wow,' Gus breathed.

She picked up the torch and inspected the space rock on her outstretched palm. Up close it was different from a normal rock, dark and slick and sparkly with tiny purple crystals embedded inside. It felt different somehow too, the weight of it in her hands. When Gus turned it over, she saw a faint crack in the rock, an almost invisible fault line.

'How did you find this?' she whispered.

Stevie hesitated before replying. 'It was when we camped here,' he said finally.

'We?' Gus repeated.

'I stayed here with my family. My mother and my little sister.'

'When?'

Stevie shrugged. 'A while ago. When we were passing through Calvary.'

'Where are they now?'

Stevie shrugged again. 'Gone,' he replied.

Gus was confused. 'You mean, they *left* you here? By yourself?'

After a pause, he looked at the stars and said, 'We were heading north. Much like you all, I suppose. Running from the city.'

'Really?' Gus replied. 'Your family did that too?'

He nodded. 'My mother was chasing work. My dad, he, uh, died when I was small.'

'I'm sorry,' Gus said.

'That's OK,' Stevie said. 'It happened a while ago.'

'How did you get here?'

'We travelled the old-fashioned way.'

'By train?' she guessed.

He smiled. 'We were travelling on foot, Gus.'

'Wow,' she said again.

She imagined his family traipsing north, Stevie and his sister waddling like ducklings behind their mother along a great stretch of highway. Gus worried about birds when she saw them walking by the road and she had the same feeling about Stevie, right then.

'When we arrived, my little sister was real sick, and my mum had to find a hospital. She got a lift to the next town, but there wasn't enough room in the truck for all of us. I was the oldest, so I—'

'You stayed behind,' Gus finished.

Stevie nodded. 'She said they'd come back for me,' he repeated. 'Once my sister was seen to, at the hospital. So, I stayed. To wait.'

Stevie didn't say it, but she knew then he was still waiting. Why hasn't his mother come back? Gus wondered. She heard the gentle trickle over the river and thought of the stones, under the skin of the water,

163

shaped and smoothed by the river — how much they had changed over time. They would hardly be recognisable from their original form now.

'What happened to them?' Gus asked quietly. 'To your family?'

'I don't actually know,' he said.

There was a fault line in his voice, like the fine crack in the space rock. Gus felt so bad for him. She wanted to take his hand and tell him it would be all right, he could come live with them in the meantime, even though they weren't friends or anything.

She looked at the fragment of meteorite, glinting in her warm hands.

'It was my mother actually,' Stevie said quietly. 'She was the one to find it. The stone.'

Being beside the river had seemed to unlock the words inside him.

'We were camping here the night she found it. That night, my mother saw what looked like a shooting star in the sky. In bed, inside our tent, around midnight she said she'd heard a loud crash and a sizzling sound as though a hot stone had hit the water.'

He paused, looking at the stone in Gus's palm. 'True as god, that's what she said. And the next morning she found this rock when she was washing my spare shirt.'

Gus was silent waiting for him to continue.

'I like to imagine it was part of a beautiful comet,' Stevie said. 'People say that comets like this place. It attracts them, or something. Some kind of cosmic force.'

He smiled.

'Wow,' Gus said once again.

She liked the way Stevie thought, beyond himself and towards the stars. 'That is cool,' she agreed.

For some reason he looked sad, then. His face closed down.

'We'd better get back,' he said.

'But we just got here,' she said, startled.

'Do you think you can remember this spot, Gus?' he asked.

'Probably,' she replied, even more confused. 'Why?'

Again, he didn't answer directly. 'Would you look after the stone for me, Gus? If, if something happened to me?'

'I — what?'

She felt uneasy at his words. 'OK,' she said. 'But I thought … you just said … what about your family? They're coming back for you, right?'

Stevie turned away from the river and began to make his way up the bank.

Gus put the rock back where she had found it, arranging the dirt so it was covered. It was a shame really, not to show anyone. Nicole, for one, would have loved to have seen this fragment of space. Gus bet they could win the science competition with it. But she wouldn't take the space rock. It belonged to Stevie. She put the final stone on top, so it couldn't be found, unless you knew where to look.

Silently Gus scrambled up the bank and followed him back home, across the headland and beneath the arbour of cane, shining the torch on the dirt track. When they reached the Starlight driveway Stevie stopped under the drive-in sign.

She stopped too and Stevie turned to face her. He smiled again, one of his lopsided grins, and she thought it was the saddest thing in the world.

Where do you go after the movie? Gus thought. Who takes care of you?

She thought of her own family in the caravan, with its lingering stink of possum, despite their cleaning efforts and being squished between her brother and sister in the double bed, while her mother snored in the single one above them. She recalled the hot fug of their shared breath, which was gross, but also made the room warm and cosy and full.

She didn't want Stevie to leave through the cane on his own. 'I can help you find your family,' Gus said. 'Tell me how I can help.'

'I don't know how, Gus. It's been too long, maybe. But you're sweet. Alice offered the same.'

Did she? Gus thought crushed. Had he taken her sister out there too? Had he shown Alice the space rock?

She heard footsteps then. She peered down the drive and made out the form of someone approaching. She supposed it was one of her family coming to check that a possum hadn't attacked her on the way back from the toilet.

'Someone's coming,' she said.

He looked at her, panicked, and she thought for a moment he might run from the spot.

'Who's there?' A voice rang out in the dark.

It wasn't one of her family, the voice belonged to a man. Could it be Henry? Or another, more sinister, ghost?

'Who's there?' the voice asked again.

167

Definitely not Henry. Gus felt her stomach flip in fear. She turned to face their pursuer. She still couldn't make out their face. She switched on the torch she had stolen from the caravan. 'Um, it's Gus Able,' she said. Her voice was high and thin in the night air. 'Projectionist at the Starlight Drive-In Movie Theatre,' she said. '(And drycleaners).'

It was probably a bad idea to identify herself. She hoped it was a moviegoer who had left something behind — a picnic basket or blanket from the movie screening. At this point she didn't even care if it was someone who wanted a refund.

'Gus?' the man's voice replied, in recognition.

He stepped into her beam of torchlight.

It was the sergeant who had ordered two helpings of dinner from her mother and who had guffawed through *Ghostbusters*. Gus felt so relieved she thought she might melt, like the green ghost in the film earlier tonight.

'What are you doing out here, all by yourself?' Sergeant Peters said.

She started to protest she wasn't alone, that everything was fine. But when she turned to indicate Stevie standing beside her, she saw he was gone.

Chapter 17

'I think this says grated cheese,' Alice said.

They were reading a list written in their mother's spidery scrawl. Mrs Able's handwriting, which had until recently communicated the messages of those who had crossed over to those still earthside, was now repurposed for shopping lists. Gus tossed a kilo of grated cheese into their trolley. The sisters were under strict instructions to stick to the list.

Gus knew they had to maintain their momentum, so the Monday after the *Ghostbusters* weekend she had risen early and tiptoed out of the caravan. Their ticket sales had improved at each of the Saturday and Sunday screenings and her mother had reported, happily, that they were now breaking even. She'd stolen up the steps to the projection room before school, intent on choosing another crowd pleaser for the coming weekend. As she opened the door she recalled the moviegoers' faces as they left the night before. They'd looked lighter somehow and perhaps a little more kind.

Gus wondered what the Calvary locals might like to see next. As she stared at the shelves of movies she recalled what Mrs Peters had said about her ballroom dancing days. It had been the first real request Gus had received as head projectionist and she decided to fulfil the woman's wish.

As she peered at the haphazardly organised films, Gus despaired. Henry didn't have a carton labelled Musicals. He did however have a box marked Romantic Comedy. In there, Gus had found a film called *Strictly Ballroom*. Gus had baulked at the romantic part, but after she'd googled it during lunch that day at school something told her to go for it.

When she had told Mum about her choice of movie, Mrs Able's eyes had lit up. Apparently it was one of her mother's favourites. She hoped Mrs Peters would like it too.

Mrs Able had spent the past few days while they were at school scribbling sample menus for the Moonbeam Cafe, themed around the movie.

On Wednesday Mrs Able had picked them up after school with a mission. She had sent her daughters to the Calvary Convenience Store to buy the ingredients in preparation for the Friday screening, while she and Artie had gone to the butcher shop. Right now, Alice was driving the trolley and reading out the list while Gus fetched the items. It was the most time the sisters had spent together in ages. Gus was glad they had a list to follow.

'Ten tins of sliced pineapple,' Alice read.

Gus made a face but followed her sister to the canned goods aisle, where they found the tins and dumped them in the trolley.

As they walked up and down the store's aisles gathering the items on their mother's list, Gus saw some familiar faces — the elderly couple who'd sat on their blanket drinking tea during *Ghostbusters* were here buying cat food. They nodded hello to the Able girls. It was strange to recognise people, Gus thought. She had read about this in books, the sense of familiarity people found in a small town, a feeling of belonging. She hadn't experienced it herself before.

The clutch of teenagers hanging out of the trucks from the other night were also in town stocking up on junk food. They stopped talking when they clocked Alice, appraising the girls silently as they went by with their laden trolley. Alice sniffed as they passed the boys and Gus was relieved to see Nathan wasn't among them.

'Five cartons of soft drink,' Alice instructed Gus in the drinks aisle.

As Gus hefted the cans of orange and lemon fizz into their trolley, she saw Sergeant Peters buying a hot roast chicken at the deli. Does he only exist to eat? Gus wondered. Perhaps this town was slow on crime. She shrank beside the fruit juices so he didn't notice her.

Though he wasn't so bad, for a police officer, she reflected. Last Friday night he had escorted her back to the caravan and insisted on speaking with her mum. They were all waiting up, her mum and her brother and sister, their mother having just dialled the local police.

Gus tried to downplay her disappearance and to her surprise the police officer took her side, calming her mother down by making her a cup of tea and the rest of them hot chocolate which he rustled up somehow from the caravan's meagre pantry. Their mother had smiled and thanked him, surreptitiously wiping at the food stain on her dress. Everything had worked out OK.

Although Gus was still mad at Stevie for running off like that. She had broken her own rule and offered friendship, then he had disappeared without even saying goodbye.

Gus was happy though to see her mother so preoccupied. She realised a total of zero strangers had knocked on their door since they'd been there. There had been no desperate bereaved appearing in their caravan, with wads of cash and vales of tears, or the more sinister types Gus had grown to dread, who wanted to exploit her mother's powers for dark purposes. Like Troy, those people wanted her mother to call up the dead for money, as far as Gus could tell.

From muffled conversations in the next room, Gus had gleaned this kind of visitor had been left out of a will or had money hidden from them. They'd come to shake down a ghost. Far more sad were the people who came to their home with sorry on their mind, which had been too long coming. Sometimes Mrs Able had summoned the ghosts and apologies had been made, but sometimes the spirits hadn't shown.

The family rift had been too wide. Always afterwards their mother had disappeared into her room, drawn and exhausted, crawling under the bedcovers. On those nights, when she hadn't the energy to emerge, Alice had looked after Gus and Artie — made them dinner and read them stories before bed, to distract them from the absence of their mother.

It was, Gus realised, in these instances that the ghosts were far kinder to her mother than the living were. They weren't so bad, she was finding, if Henry was anything to go by.

Now, rather than channelling spirits of the deceased, their mother was obsessed with bringing the ailing drive-in back to life. So far, they'd managed to keep their mother's abilities under wraps, and she seemed, well, happy.

In fact, they were all happier in Calvary, except perhaps Alice, who didn't appear to be doing as well there as she had in their past lives, in past cities and towns. There hadn't been any friends over, nor had she been popping off to sleepovers and birthday parties like she usually did.

'Three kilos of prawns and two of kabana sticks,' Alice read. 'The last items, thank goodness.'

From the drinks aisle Gus scouted out the deli counter. She saw the police officer had left with his barbecue chook, so she moved to stand by the deli cabinet. She placed her order with a lady in a hairnet, while Alice waited by their trolley.

The deli assistant took her time. While perusing the olives, Gus managed to knock over a display of nougat.

'Sorry,' she mumbled to the deli attendant, who was busy shovelling prawns into some packaging.

The woman ignored her, but just as she was finishing re-stacking the pile, something caught Gus's eye.

It was Alice, who was leaning against the tins of fruit punch in the drinks aisle.

Her sister was talking to Stevie.

Gus froze. It looked like Alice was crying.

Stevie stood opposite her, cradling his elbows. What was going on? She crept closer to them to overhear what they were saying.

He was saying, 'I'm sorry, Alice, I'm sorry.'

He looked so pained. He looked like he wanted to help her, to reassure her perhaps. He raised his hand as though he might touch her face.

Alice shrank back.

'No, please, no,' Alice whispered.

Gus looked around wildly. She needed to help. To do something. 'Hey,' she said. 'Hey, you.'

Alice turned to her, her eyes dinner plates. 'Gus?' she replied, alarmed.

She put her arm out as though to stop Gus from approaching any further. Gus stepped towards her anyway.

'Gus, I don't think you should—' her sister began.

But Gus waved her off. 'Leave her alone, Stevie,' she said.

'Gus, I'm not going to hurt her,' Stevie said slowly.

'Can't you see she's upset?' Gus replied, her voice rising. 'Just stop it, OK? Whatever it is you're doing, just stop.'

'Gus,' Alice said. 'You, you don't understand.' Her sister was visibly trembling.

'It's OK, Gus,' Stevie said.

'It's OK?' Gus repeated, her voice rising more. 'It's *OK*? Then why is Alice crying?'

Alice took Gus by the hands, then put her palms on Gus's cheeks, as though willing her to listen. 'Gus, he didn't mean to frighten me.'

'Then what did he do?' Gus asked. She turned to Stevie. 'What did you do, Stevie?'

But he wasn't there any more.

'Of course,' she said, even louder than before. 'Of course you're gone again!'

The older couple with the cat food passed by their aisle. Hearing Gus shout, they turned and gaped at the girls, then looked at each other in alarm. Gus tried to crane her neck to see where Stevie had gone.

'Gus, please,' Alice repeated. Her sister's voice was low and urgent. 'Please stop. We'll talk about this after we get home. OK?'

Gus went to protest but stopped herself because of the look in her sister's eyes.

In silence, she retrieved the prawns and the kabana from the deli counter. Wordlessly the two sisters wheeled their trolley to the checkout and paid for their groceries. All the while Gus's heart was racing.

Afterwards, they sat outside the supermarket, on a bench sticky with chewing gum. They each ate a giant lolly python and Gus clutched a bag of red frogs for Artie. These were the only deviations they had made from their mother's list. The lollies were impulse buys at the counter. Nicole's mother would be horrified at the artificial flavours and sweeteners they were currently inhaling but chewing meant they didn't have to talk.

Gus's mind was zinging. She wanted to ask Alice what was going on with Stevie. She wanted to say so much, though she didn't know where to begin. She maybe even wanted to put her arm around her sister.

A commotion a few metres away distracted her. A man had appeared by the entrance to the supermarket. He wore a smock made of a hessian bag and a necklace made of pebbles and sticks. His sandy hair was matted and he was waving his arms about and ranting loudly. He was standing next to a sandwich board that read *The end is nighe* in shaky handwriting. Gus strained to hear what he was saying.

'Ice and dirt, they say?' he called in their direction.

Gus looked at Alice to see if they should respond. Her sister had her head in her hands.

'More like fire and sin!' the man in the potato sack continued. 'Mark my words, this comet is the devil. Riley's will be the end of us,' he called.

Gus looked at Alice in alarm. She didn't appear to be very concerned about the ranting man in the hessian bag.

'Check that out,' she said, nudging Alice with her elbow.

Alice glanced over and shrugged. Clearly, she had bigger things on her mind.

'Riley's is coming for us!' the man shouted.

Gus was relieved to see their mother hurrying towards them, Artie in tow.

'Come on, girls,' Mrs Able called. 'I've got to get these sausages in the fridge.'

The two sisters rose from the bench just as the automatic doors of the supermarket opened. Through them strolled Sergeant Peters, stuffing his face with chips. Was eating his second job? Gus wondered. He stopped short when he saw their mother.

'Delphine, hi,' he said, brushing salt and vinegar crumbs from his chin and collar. His face flushed salmon pink.

'Hello, Terry,' their mother said shyly.

Alice looked at them both, appalled.

'Beware the comet!' shouted the man in the sack.

Their mother made a startled noise and Artie cracked up laughing.

'Delphine, let me handle this,' said Sergeant Peters.

He approached the man cautiously, as though approaching an unfriendly dog. 'Hey, Joe,' he soothed. 'Easy mate.'

'Terry?' replied the man in the sack cloth suspiciously.

'Yeah,' said Terry. 'Want to put the sign down, mate?'

'Riley's Comet is hell!' screamed Joe. He advanced on the police officer, sign held high.

Their mother cried out in alarm.

'I've got this,' the sergeant said to their mother, shielding his face from Joe's sign with his hands. 'You get everyone home. I'll see you on Friday for the movie. Pick a good one, Gus!'

Gus nodded, unable to look away. The Able family began to back away with their shopping. She thought about calling the police, but then she remembered Sergeant Peters *was* the police. She hoped he had things in hand.

People are really getting worked up about this comet, Gus thought. But then, she reflected, she and Alice appeared to have bigger problems.

Chapter 18

The next day after school had finished, following their eventful shopping trip in town, Gus found herself hanging out down by the screen under the mango tree.

Worryingly, Stevie hadn't appeared all afternoon, although she had hung out by the screen in plain sight and kept her eyes peeled for him at school. She needed to find out what had happened with Alice. She had no choice, as Alice herself was avoiding Gus today. In fact, her sister didn't appear to be speaking to anyone at school or at home. Instead Alice had wafted around like well, a ghost, pale and silent. She had that *don't even start* look again.

'What's with you today?' Nicole had asked earlier in science class. 'You seem kind of distracted.'

They had been given time in class by Ms McKenzie to work on their comet projects. Gus shrugged and tried to focus on what Nicole was saying.

Her science project partner went on to explain how a complicated-sounding chemical reaction would mimic the effect of a comet. Apparently, they needed to combine dry ice, water, rubbing alcohol and dirt.

'Did you find some nice gravel?' Nicole had asked.

Gus had nodded. Privately she thought it sounded like a recipe for sludge. But then, that's what a comet was, in essence, if you thought about it.

'It's going to be amazing,' Nicole said confidently.

'Now, class,' Ms McKenzie had said as she wrapped up the lesson. 'The best time to view Riley's Comet in our part of the world, or the eastern horizon, is the winter sky at night, when the moon has disappeared and the sky is darkest. That's only around three weeks away.'

There had been a ripple of excitement through the room, although Gus hadn't shared her classmates' enthusiasm.

A kid raised his hand.

'Yes, Frank?' their teacher responded.

'Miss, are we all going to get beamed up? My dad said this comet is the second coming.'

'I hope not, Frank,' Ms McKenzie said. 'Now class, turn to page thirty-eight in your science textbook ...'

Gus recalled the strange man with the sandwich board outside the supermarket. Did he really think they were going to be wiped out by the thing? She was of the opinion that the greater tragedy on Wednesday at the supermarket was that it had been the last time she saw Stevie.

As evening descended Gus trudged back to the Moonbeam for dinner, bothered by the fact Stevie was still a no-show. She had to find out what was going on between him and Alice. She hoped he'd turn up for the movie tomorrow.

Chapter 19

On Friday night at six fifty pm the drive-in was almost half full.

It's a kind of miracle, Gus thought. She felt a little giddy as she watched Alice dispensing movie tickets in her booth from the projection room window. Tonight's takings should be good. Everyone — her mother, Henry and even Deirdre — would be pleased.

Earlier they'd sampled the pizzas their mother had made for the Moonbeam customers, as the family gathered for their usual pre-movie pep talk. The Supreme version had pretty much every ingredient she and Alice had bought at Calvary Convenience Store on it: prawns, tinned pineapple and kabana stick. Miraculously it wasn't too bad. An acquired taste, perhaps, but definitely sellable, at least to the most brave-hearted and iron-stomached patrons.

'Did you know a digital movie projector costs around a hundred thousand dollars?' their mother had remarked after she'd checked everything was in order for screening *Strictly Ballroom*. Mrs Able sounded a bit giddy also.

Gus shook her head that she did not know that.

'That's not including all the other upgrades we'd have to make,' their mother mused.

'But we'd need a really long lease to do anything like that, wouldn't we?' Alice asked.

It was the first time Gus had heard her speak to anyone since the supermarket incident two days earlier. Deirdre had been right. Alice seemed to have a good head for maths and helping their mother with the business.

In fact, Deirdre had shown up that night, despite her warning two weeks earlier after the grand re-opening. Gus recognised her maroon Statesman, the wide boxy car, which sat centre front row. Gus swallowed her worry. Deirdre was just curious, she told herself. She hoped the Director of the local Amateur Dramatic Society wasn't spying on them.

'I suppose you're right,' their mother had said to Alice. 'But perhaps it can be done, one day.'

Gus had to agree with her sister they were perhaps getting a bit ahead of themselves. She admired her mother's ambition, but that figure was a lot of money. It seemed very out of reach.

At six fifty-five pm, Henry had not shown his face in the projection room. She had counted on him showing up to double check she had loaded the film correctly. Her worst nightmare would be loading the film backwards or accidentally damaging the soundtrack fused to the picture negatives, or, heaven forbid, the projector itself breaking down.

She felt nervous about the equipment working, not to mention the choice of film. She was relieved when she saw Sergeant Peters arrive and settle his mother in her usual spot, with assistance from Artie. At least one person should be happy with my programming, Gus thought.

At two minutes to seven, Henry drifted in. 'All set, sport?'

'I think so,' Gus said nervously.

It was the first time she'd prepared the projector by herself.

With a practised eye, Henry reviewed her efforts. 'Looks ship shape,' he remarked.

Gus felt herself smile.

Henry turned his attention to the drive-in below. 'Good crowd,' he remarked. 'I reckon you've got a knack for this.'

'Um, thanks,' said Gus, surprised and pleased by the compliment at the same time.

At seven pm, her hands shaking, Gus began playing *Strictly Ballroom*.

'Ah this one,' Henry said as the first scenes unspooled. 'This is one of Deirdre's favourite movies. Maybe that's where it all went wrong with her,' he mused. 'Might be where she got her taste for high drama.'

Almost immediately Gus was drawn into the story and the lives of the two main characters, Scott and Fran, as they navigated preparations for the Pan Pacific Dance Championships. Gus couldn't decide what she liked more about the film, the swishy costumes or the over-the-top story.

Despite not being a fan of romance, it was hard to ignore the charming way the professional Scott was falling for ugly duckling Fran, who was a total beginner. Fran was actually a terrific dancer in the end and the story was so silly and fun Gus almost forgave them for falling in love. The way Scott and Fran gazed at each other as they danced on the roof around a washing line strung with underpants, beneath a giant Coca-Cola sign, reminded her of the way Stevie had looked at Alice in the light of the Starlight screen, just a week earlier.

A thought jolted her. Were they in love too, like Scott and Fran from the movie? The thought gave Gus a strange feeling in her tummy. She forced herself to concentrate on her screening. She was alone in the projection room. At some point Henry had slipped out.

When the movie ended, Gus took a moment to look at the crowd. Mrs Peters' eyes were trained on the projection room window and they were shining. Alice was still sitting in the ticket booth alone. Stevie hadn't shown tonight.

Chapter 20

The following Wednesday found Gus hanging around the Starlight screen again.

She hoped if she chose the right thing to show at the Starlight, Stevie would show up. She needed to confront him about what had happened with Alice, because her sister still wasn't talking. She was also hoping he would provide her with more movie guidance. She had to get the next selection right, to bring even more people in, while they were on a roll with their audience. She had to choose something cool. Something with adventure and fantasy. Something with a magical fictional universe and a person who saves herself, all of the things she and Stevie had agreed were best about stories. But it was nearly four pm and he hadn't appeared. She had to place the ad in the paper before five. She wished she'd thought to google this at school. She sighed and tramped up the stairs to the projection room. Maybe Henry might have a suggestion.

This afternoon, the door to the projection room creaked as usual when Gus opened it. There was no hint of Henry's presence. She would have to summon him then.

She strode to the window and flung open the curtain. Dust flew everywhere like a meteor shower in miniature. Gus coughed theatrically.

Henry did not appear.

She switched on the projector and heard the now-familiar hum as it set to warming up. She thought about handling some film with her bare hands, putting her sticky fingerprints over the frames. Surely that would rouse him. But she couldn't bring herself to do it.

Below her in the cafe she could hear the sound of the freezer opening and closing, and boxes of drinks and snacks being unpacked. Her mother had enlisted Artie to help her do a stocktake for the coming weekend. Panic rose up in her. There would be no screening if she didn't pick a movie very soon.

Gus moved to the wall of metal cabinets and began to rifle through the films.

Surely the clanging would summon Henry out from wherever he was. She didn't like to think too much about where that might be. Even his rickety hut by the river, where he'd apparently lived pre-disappearance, seemed preferable to the shadowy spirit haunts her mind conjured: dark corridors and brambly thickets where the lost and damned roamed. She reminded herself she didn't know what Henry wanted or what sort of unfinished business he had.

She thought of Henry's old manual and the movies listed there in his neat handwriting. The book was stuffed with everything there was to know about the Starlight, and the town of Calvary. Maybe she would find another idea for a movie in there. She retrieved the manual from its spot on the second shelf and opened it.

This time, a bunch of loose papers fell out, everything discoloured with age or mouldy from having gone through countless wet seasons. Someone had been poking around in Henry's manual here. Deirdre perhaps? Her car had been at the last screening. Gus decided to take the manual and keep it in the caravan, safe from Deirdre's prying or interference.

Gus retrieved the papers from the floor. There were more stories cut out from the newspaper about movie celebrities visiting the Starlight, and documents which had words on them like deed and title, as well as more old photos of the place. One photo stood out, a picture of a couple in 1950s clothes, she in a gingham dress and he in short shorts and square glasses. Between them stood a boy in a sailor suit. They were posed beneath the Starlight sign. Gus guessed this was Henry and his parents when they first bought the place.

There was also a photo of a younger Deirdre, in her teens, at work in the Moonbeam, wearing acid wash jeans and a shiny purple blouse with shoulder pads. Her light brown hair was all teased out and her fringe was gelled into a bubble over her forehead. She held a tray with a milkshake on it in one of those old tin cups. Deirdre was right, she had been starlet material. Gus almost felt sorry for her then. Almost.

Gus put the photos back, feeling bad for trespassing on Henry's personal life. As she slotted the loose bits and pieces of Henry's life back in the book, another article snipped from a newspaper caught her eye.

Dear son missing the headline said. *Family seeking any information from residents of Calvary.* Gus scanned the article quickly. Apparently the family were itinerants who had stayed around Calvary for a short time, looking for work. They had left abruptly for medical reasons and then returned to town to collect their son, who had disappeared in their brief absence. A quote from the mother described her son as a 'good boy of thirteen and kind to his little sister Gracie'. There wasn't a photo or date, that had been snipped away.

Gus stuffed the sad article back in the book with the photos and property documents. Why had Henry kept all this stuff? Perhaps this was his final business, Gus thought, making the book for his daughter, the heir to the Starlight empire. Maybe that was why Henry had appeared to her, for help finishing it. The book still had some blank pages. The sad thing was, Deirdre had made it clear she wanted none of it.

And Henry had died before the manual was finished and before they could repair the row.

Gus's head was spinning, but now was not the time to reflect on ghost business. She needed to choose a movie. She forced her mind back to the projection room and read the film titles aloud. Some of them sounded familiar and made her think of Gran.

When Gus and Alice were small, Gran had babysat them while their mother plied her services as a medium in a local arcade, a galley of empty shops. On these occasions, Gran had told them stories about when she had been young. She had spoken about going to the pictures often, which was what they called the cinema in the olden days. Gran had gone with her friends, and then with Pop while he was alive. Her favourite movies, Gran recalled, had singing and dancing numbers and actresses with wobbly soprano voices and perfectly coiffed hair. She probably would have loved *Strictly Ballroom*, Gus thought.

Gus felt a longing to see Gran again. It had been so long since they had visited, ever since Gran had returned to the farm after her last stint at the clinic. Gus wiped her eyes and shook her head to shake out the memory of her gran in that white-walled place. She wondered if the clinic had cured her. Did Gran see ghosts any more? Had she escaped the Able curse?

Her hand lit on a film canister with a familiar title: *Picnic at Hanging Rock*.

Gran had spoken about this movie once, Gus recalled. It had been in hushed tones, laced with caution, when it had played on daytime TV at the farm. Gran had switched it off midway through.

'What happens in the movie, Gran?' the younger Gus had asked.

Her grandmother had thought for a while before replying. 'Oh, nothing terribly much,' concluded Gran. 'But it's dreadful anyway,' she cautioned.

'I don't understand,' Gus had said.

'It's an enigma,' Gran explained.

Gus had no idea what that meant, but the word conjured images of spaceships, wormholes in space, and sailors being swallowed by beasts at sea.

She turned the canister over. Well now she *had* to see it. She went downstairs to the cafe and dialled the newspaper to place the ad. She took Henry's manual with her for safekeeping.

Chapter 21

'And then the comet went pew, pew, pew, bang, crash!' shouted Artie throwing himself to the ground, schoolbag and all.

'Did it really?' Gus replied absentmindedly.

She helped him up, but Artie wasn't finished.

'And the meteor exploded everywhere! Like a fireball, arghhhhhh!'

He threw himself to the ground again and mimed exploding into bits.

'Wow,' said Gus, still distracted. 'That sounds ... intense.'

'It was,' Artie informed her. 'Mr Grieg said he could see the space rock crashing into their front paddock from his verandah. He told me it was Riley's Comet he saw. He was only a little kid at the time.'

'Gosh, how old is your teacher, anyway? No wonder he teaches history. He must have walked with the dinosaurs. Anyway, get up, Artie,' Gus told him. 'We'll be late for school.'

Up ahead, Alice stalked in front of them. They still hadn't spoken about what had happened with Stevie at the store, though it had been over a week ago. Gus felt the space stretching between them. It was a lovely almost-winter day, but up ahead their sister's shoulders sagged as they approached the school gate.

'Gus,' said Artie.

'Yes?' she replied.

A serious look settled on his face. 'Do you think Riley's Comet will fall out of the sky?'

His brown eyes were a puddle of worry. He had caught the comet bug, too. Curse the man with the sign outside the store, Gus thought. She realised she had overlooked her little brother. She had been so absorbed in her own problems, not to mention Alice's, that she hadn't considered Artie might be anxious about the strange events of late also.

Gus brushed gravel and dust from the ground off her brother's uniform and helped him shoulder his schoolbag again. She gave him a little nudge through the school gate.

'If Riley's Comet does fall,' she said, 'Optimus Prime will protect us.'

Artie brightened, recalling the fact Transformers had indeed saved the earth on numerous occasions prior.

'Haha, Riley's is gunna fall on your head!' Artie replied.

He kissed Gus on the arm and dashed off to join his Year One posse.

She smiled as she watched him, but her smile disappeared when she saw Alice try to pass through a group of Year Seven boys into their school building. The boys were pressing all around her sister like a footy scrum. Gus approached them cautiously.

The boys were laughing and jeering at her sister, like they had at the drive-in. But this time she was the one moving and they weren't letting her through. And there was an audience. It seemed the whole playground had stopped to watch.

There was a roaring in her ears and her face felt hot.

Alice put her arms over her face and pushed through the scrum of kids, propelling herself up the steps and towards her classroom. Gus couldn't see her sister's face but knew by the way Alice held herself that she was trying not to cry.

'She's so weird,' Frank from Gus's class said. 'The way she's always talking to herself?'

'Yeah, and looking over her shoulder like she's being followed or something? Even though there's no one there. So creepy,' she overheard another kid say.

It was Nathan, the same boy who tormented Nicole. The boys laughed and slapped each other's backs all the way to class, Gus fuming in their wake.

She should have spoken up. She should have chased after her sister. But something had stopped her. Gus felt so confused. She'd wanted to save Alice. It had been such a strange sight, seeing her usually popular sister being bullied like that, but she hadn't quite known how to help. Alice had crossed over some invisible state line, to a place Gus hadn't yet been and one where she didn't speak the language.

Chapter 22

Gus didn't get to talk to her sister about what had happened after school though, because Alice was nowhere to be found.

Gus waited in the Moonbeam Cafe after she and Artie had scoffed stale but generously jam-coated scones for afternoon tea. Their mother was too busy using the calculator on her phone and writing down figures in a notebook to join them.

When her sister didn't show, Gus went to check the projection room, though Alice had not ever poked so much as her nose in the place since Deirdre's first tour, as far as Gus could tell. Alice wasn't among the dust motes or film canisters. Her sister was nowhere to be found.

Only as Gus was setting one of the aluminium tables under the cafe awning for their dinner that night did she see her sister, coming home through the canefields. Had she seen Stevie again? Gus wondered. It didn't seem like a good thing for Alice to do.

At the table, Alice ate slowly, taking mouse-like bites of the homemade dinner their mother plonked down. It did not appear to have come from a box or a packet, which was unusual.

Gus watched her sister anxiously for any signs of distress. Artie slurped noisily at his glass of lime cordial.

'So, Gus,' their mother said brightly, 'what do you think you'd like to do next Friday?'

'Pardon?' asked Gus, taken aback by the question.

'For your birthday, darling,' her mother gently chided. 'You didn't think I'd forgotten, did you?'

'Um,' Gus replied.

Gus had actually. She'd almost forgotten herself. Her birthdays had always been non-events. There hadn't ever been anyone to invite. She squished in a mouthful of mince and peas. If she were on a quiz show and had to guess what dinner was for prize money, she would choose savoury mince.

Her mother was eyeing Gus carefully. 'Turning twelve is a special event in the lives of the Able women,' she said. 'It would be nice to celebrate the occasion.'

Alice appeared to choke on a mouthful of dinner.

'Women,' Artie chortled.

He stuck a green bean up his nose. Their mother ignored him.

You don't say, Gus thought. Since leaving the city, in technically her twelfth year in the world, everything had gone wrong. For a start, she hadn't seen ghosts before now. 'Special' was the wrong word probably, though. 'Weird' covered it better, Gus thought.

'Would you like to have a pizza party?' her mother probed. 'We've got the movie thing covered. Perhaps you could invite some people from school.'

Gus didn't know how to break it to her mother that she only hung out with one person at school, a kid the other students called 'Kale Girl', and that was only because they were science partners. Surely this was not surprising, however, given her track record at previous schools. Unlike Alice, Gus thought.

Except for now.

She looked over at her sister, whose face had gone red with the effort of eating dinner. Suddenly,

Gus felt mad at her sister. Why did she get to be all mysterious and left alone, while Gus was expected to spill her guts?

'I guess Alice would know something about it,' she heard herself saying. 'Tell us, Alice, what's so great about growing up, anyway?'

Alice looked at her, murderous. She shoved back her chair, the legs scraping on the concrete, and rose from the table. She strode off in the direction she had come from, out the door and through the cane paddocks and beyond, to who knew where.

Gus rose, a sick feeling in her stomach, to follow her sister. But her mother reached across the table and put a hand on Gus's arm, indicating she shouldn't go after her.

Chapter 23

It had been late when Alice had slipped through the
door of the caravan like an alley cat, and lain down
in her spot in the double bed the Able children shared.
It had seemed to Gus her sister was made of barely
anything, of less than air, so little did she feel Alice's
weight beside her.

Gus was so relieved when her sister came in she
hardly dared breathe. Earlier, lying beside the oblivious,
snoring Artie, who cuddled his Transformer, she had
worried she had driven her sister away for good.

She had heard her mother in the single bed rise and
peer out the caravan window several times. She sighed
when she sat down on the bed and the mattress springs
had sighed with her. Mrs Able's behaviour at dinner
had been odd, Gus thought. Why had she peered so

intently at her middle child when asking about her birthday celebrations? She hoped her mother wasn't planning to have 'The Talk' with her soon. When Alice had turned twelve a year and a half back, her mother had trotted her off to a cafe for a milkshake and 'The Talk'. Alice had locked herself in her bedroom for the rest of the day on their return.

Her thoughts chased each other as she wondered where Alice had slipped off to. An hour after her sister reappeared, Gus was still awake, restless but unable to turn over without disturbing her bedmates.

A light flared on and the caravan interior was lit up like a TV studio. Gus sat up in bed. Had someone turned on the floodlights?

Everyone else in the caravan woke with a start but continued to lie in their beds, stunned like the fish on ice in the store deli.

From her spot wedged between her siblings, Gus clambered over Artie and, pushing the paisley curtains aside, saw a radiant glow outside the window. There was a fire by the drive-in.

The projector, Gus recalled in a panic. Henry had warned her she should not let it overheat. Had she turned it off? Had she forgotten to take out the film reel from the projector after the last movie screening?

Unless it was Riley's Comet. Could it have descended on them like the man outside the store had forewarned? She felt light-headed with the thought.

Gus felt her mother's presence beside her, the sleeve of her cotton nightie brushing Gus's arm.

'They're burning off,' her mother said. 'The sugarcane is ready for harvesting.'

Gus exhaled in relief. She hadn't left the projector running and inadvertently set them all on fire. It wasn't the comet.

'Cool!' said Artie. 'Can we go watch?'

'If we must,' said their mother sleepily. 'But don't go any further than the driveway. I'll come with you.'

Artie shot out the caravan door and their mother followed close in her nightie. Gus moved to the door too. She had never seen such a big fire and something drew her to its orange pulse. It's like a spaceship coming to collect us, Gus thought.

'Coming to watch the fire, Alice?' she asked.

Her sister didn't reply. Instead, she turned her head to the wall.

Chapter 24

Come Friday, a respectable line snaked from the ticket booth and down the gravel driveway of the drive-in. Tonight it appeared they would be almost two-thirds full.

Alice sat in the ticket booth, wan and untalkative, but still in possession of her maths skills, taking money, making change and dispensing tickets. Artie was in his element, guiding vehicles to their allocated spot, tuning speakers and flashing his torch about with a sense of self-importance. At six forty-five pm the drive-in was almost full. Cars were lined up in neat satisfying rows facing the screen. It looked like they would be almost sold out of spots.

Their mother was cooking up a storm in the cafe, with several pots on the boil. The cabinet on the counter was full of sausage rolls, Chiko rolls and hot roast rolls. The drinks fridge was fully stocked.

Even Nicole and her mother rocked up on their tandem bike with a crystal dangling from the handlebars and a sticker on the frame proclaiming *Magic Happens*. Gus noticed they steered clear of the cafe food. They'd probably had green bowls for dinner, which as far as Gus could tell contained radishes and grass and not much else.

Henry hadn't shown, but she expected him to materialise at any moment. He always had so far. Unless he had forgotten? she wondered.

Looking at the crowd below, Gus felt quite proud of herself. She had chosen a movie that had got the punters in and set everything up all on her own.

From the projection room window, she saw the scorched paddock beyond their fence line. While they'd been watching the fire consume the stalks of sugarcane, small creatures had fled from the rows in terror. Gus had seen snakes and lizards as well as wallabies and even a cat fleeing the flames. Black smoke had risen above the cane-flower tips and for a moment it had been hard to breathe. Smoke had filled their lungs and as she coughed and wiped her watering eyes, Gus fancied she'd seen a figure emerge from the cane.

The person was lanky and, unlike the fleeing animals, had moved unhurriedly, as though the fire at his back didn't bother him at all. For a moment her heart stopped. Troy, she thought. He had pursued them up the coast and finally found them. She'd rubbed her eyes and stared at the figure.

'Come on,' their mother had said. 'Let's go back inside.'

For a moment, Mrs Able looked shaken too, but she recovered quickly, putting a hand on Gus's shoulder.

'We've seen enough,' her mother had coaxed. 'Let's go back to bed.'

Eyes still watering, Gus had retreated to the caravan with Artie and her mum, banging the door shut behind them. They were treated to a showstopper light display on the caravan wall as the fire continued to burn outside and, with the last of the reflected flames flickering on their wall, Gus finally fell asleep.

After they'd burned the cane, the farmer had sent his harvester and haul-out trucks to cut and load the blackened crop. They had made quick work of the task, stripping the paddock bare until only charred earth and the smell of burned sugar remained.

The sound of someone clearing their throat startled Gus. Henry had arrived. She glanced at the clock. Six fifty pm. Ten minutes to show time. She needed to hustle and load the film.

'I know, I know,' Gus said. 'In fifty years as a projectionist you've always started on time—'

She turned to face the projectionist.

But it was not Henry.

Instead, Deirdre stood in the doorway, fresh from rehearsals, in a sweeping royal blue frock. She also wore a displeased look on her face.

'Miss Cronk, hi,' Gus said, confused. 'Are you looking for my mum? She's serving people at the Moonbeam.'

'I can *see* that, Augusta. I couldn't get a *moment* in private to speak with her. There were a whole *bunch* of locals lining up for prawn *cocktails*. *Disgusting*, if you ask *me*.'

Gus wasn't sure if Deirdre was referring to the locals or the menu item.

'Delphine certainly is taking *liberties*,' Deirdre

continued. 'She's ditched *my* menu and gone *completely* off script.'

'I'm sorry,' Gus said, confused. 'Um, what?'

'Oh, *don't* play disingenuous with *me*,' Deirdre snorted.

'Dis-in-what? Miss Cronk — I — I have to start the film,' Gus said.

She was feeling a little panicked. She had to load *Picnic at Hanging Rock* in the projector and her hands were shaking.

'Oh, we have time enough for *that*,' said Deirdre, waving her hand airily. 'So, what *were* you thinking, Gus? To program this film on the opening night of *Les Misérables*. *Stealing* my audience! Do *tell*.'

Gus opened her mouth and closed it again. She did not know what to say.

'And did you *really* think you would succeed? Did you really think you could *revive the Starlight*? And outdo *my* efforts, after *all* I've tried to *do* for this place. For this *town*.'

Gus looked out the window. It appeared they had succeeded in getting people to come here again. You only had to count the cars and get Alice's box office tally. It was a question of pure maths.

'I, well, I ...' Gus stammered.

The truth was she *had* thought that. And hadn't Deirdre herself asked them to do that very thing when they first arrived? Hadn't that been what she'd tasked them with?

'*Well*? What do you have to *say* for yourself?' Deirdre demanded.

'Um,' Gus said. 'I guess they like what we do. The movies and the meal deals ...'

'*Really*,' Deirdre said. 'Oh, isn't that *sweet*.'

'I — I —' Gus tried.

'And because they've all come *here*, instead of to my theatre production, all these *locals*, I suppose you think that you *belong* now, or something? That you've won your *place* here? You and your ... *unusual* ... family.'

'Um,' said Gus. 'Oh,' she said again.

'That's so *adorable*,' Deirdre purred. 'But you're *wrong*, Augusta. As soon as I saw your *family* arrive, I knew there was something *odd* about you. You're *hiding* something and *I'm* going to find out what it *is*. And when I *do*, I'm going to tell *everyone*. And then your little reign as *Screen Queen* will be *over*.'

Gus swallowed. They needed this. Mrs Able would

be devastated if they were turned out. She had made so many plans.

'It was an innocent *mistake*, I suppose. To think that you *belonged* somehow. I *hate* to be the one to break this to you Gus, but you will *never* be accepted here. Not you, nor your feckless *mother* or your … glassy-eyed *sister* or your over-stimulated *brother*. *None* of you.'

Gus blinked. Deirdre continued.

'I'll show *you*, for stealing *my* audience. The very townspeople I served chicken *chippies* to, for years! That's not even a real *food*! Those people *owe* me this. My moment in the *spotlight*. I'll show *you*. You tell your *mother*, Augusta. I'll find out what you're *running* from. It'll serve your family *right* for trying to upstage *me*!'

Gus swallowed the stone that had turned up in her throat. She didn't know how to reply. It was almost seven pm and she needed to start the movie, but she didn't know if she'd be able to see the buttons on the projector with her eyes leaking the way they were.

Then Henry appeared, behind Deirdre, in the doorway, just for a moment. He stood behind his daughter, who did not see him. He held a finger to his lips, indicating that Gus shouldn't say a word. Then he vanished back down the stairs.

'So *naive*, darling, to think you could succeed over me. This declaration of my father's death is taking *far* too long and you've been a thorn in my *side*, but I will *prevail*,' Deirdre continued.

She was practically ranting now, delivering her own personal monologue to an invisible audience. It didn't seem to matter to her whether Gus was there or not.

'I'll admit I have a lot on my *plate*, with *Les Mis* now in production and the costume mistress *quitting* and taking the costumes. I had to run up *pantaloons* for the *extras* last night, in *addition* to remembering my *lyrics*. But *mark my words*, you *will not win*. You will not *beat* me. You and your vaudeville act of a *family* must never forget who *owns* this place.'

'Henry,' Gus managed. 'Henry owns the Starlight,' she said.

A sour look passed over Deirdre's face. 'That's a *technicality*, darling. Don't backchat *me*. It will belong to me soon *enough*, when my father is declared dead. Go on, *show* your little movie then. But don't you forget who *owns* this place and the *caravan* your mother keeps you all in. As I said, I will *prevail*.'

She left in a huff. Gus watched her go down the stairs. There was no further sign of Henry. But the town was waiting.

Her hands still trembling, Gus started the film at one minute past seven. She felt Henry would forgive her this time.

Chapter 25

'Spectators, behold!' said Nicole.

They stood in front of the class. Nicole was wearing clear goggles and washing-up gloves while brandishing a bag of dry ice. Beside her, Gus, also in gloves, held a mixing bowl borrowed from the Moonbeam Cafe containing dirt, gravel, hand sanitiser, corn starch and vinegar. On the teacher's desk sat Nicole's pink hairdryer, which was plugged in and ready to go.

'Behold and marvel,' Nicole continued. 'The comet cometh!'

It was their turn to present their science assignment and Nicole was taking the opportunity very seriously. She had been right, the other teams before them had offered garbage bag–covered balls with streamers attached. They had read notes straight from Wikipedia, assignments which had been pronounced as completely unoriginal by Nicole.

They, on the other hand, were apparently going to do a proper demonstration, like actual NASA scientists. Nicole had adopted a ye olde worlde accent for their presentation.

'And now behold, I will add the smoke to the nucleus. Spectators, prepare to be bamboozled!' Nicole announced. 'Gus,' she cued in a whisper, 'bring forth the bowl.'

As prompted, Gus brought the bowl and its contents closer to Nicole and her dry ice. She had no idea what was going to happen. Perhaps we should have practised this at home, she thought belatedly.

Nicole slowly and theatrically poured the dry ice into Gus's mixing bowl. The concoction began to hiss and bubble.

'Er, stand back, class,' Ms McKenzie said.

Dirty clouds formed around the girls as the mixture in the bowl began to clump and release smoke.

'Do not be alarmed, people, the smoke is merely the product of the reaction, causing gas to escape,' Nicole assured everyone.

'Yeah, causing gas like your lunch, Kale Girl,' one of the footy boys sniggered.

Nicole ignored him. The dirty clump of mush in the bowl began to billow more smoke. Using gloves, she began to mould the material into a ball.

'Witness the nucleus! The heart of a comet is made of ice and frozen gas as well as dirt particles,' she explained as she worked.

The more she worked with the mixture the more it smoked, until their comet was billowing a dirty great cloud.

'Um, Nicole?' Gus whispered.

Ms McKenzie began to cough. 'Girls, I think we get the idea,' she said.

'Maybe I should open a window?' Gus offered.

'But we're not done,' Nicole protested. 'Next up we have to show how the comet produces jet streams as it enters our atmosphere,' she said. 'Gus, apply the heat,' she instructed.

'Nicole, I don't think we should—'

'Gus! The hairdryer, remember?' Nicole prompted, passing the smoking ball of mixture from hand to hand. 'Quickly! It's getting quite hot now.'

Her shoulders sinking, Gus retrieved the hairdryer and aimed it at the smoking mass in Nicole's hands. The thing began to spark jets of gas.

'Gus! Nicole! That's enough, now!' their teacher said, switching the hairdryer off at the power point.

Particles of dry ice began to break off Nicole's comet. One shot out and just missed hitting her on the forehead.

'Drop that thing in the bin,' Ms McKenzie commanded.

Gus retrieved the comet nucleus from a stunned Nicole and threw it in the rubbish. It had almost burned through her gloves it was so hot. The comet fizzled out but the smoke haze persisted.

'Class, it's time to evacuate. Assemble on the football oval, please. Gus, take Nicole to the first aid room by the principal's office. I'll be along to have a word with you both shortly.'

Ms McKenzie pressed the break-glass alarm by her desk, and bells began to reverberate through the classroom and also Gus's head.

The whole class rose and stampeded to the door. Gus took Nicole's hand as Ms McKenzie shooed them out.

'Come with me,' she said to Nicole, leading her out the classroom door.

Next time, she thought, we should submit our assignment online. It seemed like it would be safer somehow.

Chapter 26

If Gus thought her mother being called up to the principal's office, to be informed her daughter had helped set their classroom on fire was bad, what awaited her at home was worse.

It took Gus the afternoon and most of the evening to realise Alice had gone.

While their sister wasn't there after school to share the peach-blossom cakes their mother had made, that wasn't unusual. Alice didn't always join them for afternoon tea, although, come to think of it, Gus hadn't seen her on the school oval after they'd all been evacuated from their classrooms today either.

Alice didn't join them for dinner that evening, but it was only when Gus was brushing her teeth in the drive-in toilet block that she realised her sister's toothbrush was missing from the jar they usually kept them in.

A quick search in the cabinet under the sink revealed Alice's toiletry bag was also gone.

Panic flooded through Gus. Her sister was gone. She had vanished, just like Stevie.

Gus spat out her toothpaste and ran back to the caravan, her thongs slapping against the concrete path. 'Mum,' she said out of breath to Mrs Able, who was adding up receipts at the tiny caravan banquette table. 'Mum!'

Mrs Able glanced up, looking mildly put out that her calculations had been interrupted.

'Alice is missing,' Gus informed her mother urgently.

Mrs Able looked at her middle child as though she wasn't quite sure how to reply. Why wasn't her mother jumping to her feet? Why wasn't she calling the police, or racing out to look for her daughter, combing the paddocks, or raising a search party in town?

Her mother looked over at Artie, who was watching a local news story about comet trackers on their tiny television. The show featured people from Calvary wearing suits of aluminium foil, who chased comet sightings in their beat-up trucks. Some of the trucks were mounted with a radio dish, presumably to communicate with those from outer space. Why was everyone in town so obsessed by that stupid comet? Gus fumed. Her sister's disappearance was a far more important enigma and her mother's apparent lack of concern was unsettling.

'Well,' added Gus anxiously, 'are we going out to look for her?'

Instead of replying, her mother put her finger to her lips, indicating Gus should hush. Mrs Able got up from her accounting and gestured that Gus should follow her outside.

Her mother closed the door so Artie wouldn't overhear and they sat squashed together on the aluminium steps of the caravan. There wasn't a moon tonight, though the stars glinted in the inky backdrop of the sky mischievously, Gus thought.

'I know where she is, Gus,' her mother said.

'You do?' Gus replied.

'Yes. In fact, I sent her there.'

Gus breathed out in relief. 'Alice is safe,' she said.

'If you consider Gran's house, with its excessive levels of crochet and farm cats, safe, then yes, she's fine,' her mother replied, smiling. 'I put her on the bus myself while you and Artie were at school. It will do Alice good to be away from this place for a while.'

Gus felt the terror that had been sitting on her shoulders dissolve.

Her mother paused. She appeared not to know what to say next. Then she just said it anyway. 'Alice hasn't taken to this town — this new life — as well as you, Gus.'

Gus nearly fell off the steps in surprise. She scrutinised her mother's face in the moonlight. Mum appeared to be serious, even despite the fiasco in science class today.

'I'm proud of you,' her mother added.

Gus's jaw dropped. No one had ever said that to her, least of all her mother.

'What?' her mother asked, smiling. 'You've turned this dead horse drive-in around, Gus. You've worked hard to learn how to use that projector and you've been clever in how you've used it. Not everyone could do that.'

If only Deirdre thought so too, Gus thought darkly. She hadn't told her mother about Deirdre's visit to the projection room the previous Friday. There had been so much happening she didn't want to worry her mother any more. But not even the Director (and lead actress) of the local Amateur Dramatic Society could dampen her mood, now that she knew Alice was OK and that her mother was actually proud of her.

Gus had to admit she'd had some help though. Both Henry and Stevie had steered her in the right direction when choosing crowd favourites. *Stevie*. His name gave her a pang under the ribs.

'Alice left because of a boy, didn't she?' she asked into the night.

Her mother turned to her sharply. 'How do you know about that?'

'I've seen them together, Mum.'

Before Gus could ask her mother more, headlights from the road dazzled her for a moment. Someone was idling at the entrance to the Starlight driveway. The driver probably just made a wrong turn, Gus thought.

But the headlights grew brighter as the car turned into their drive, trained on the cafe and the caravan. The driver only cut them with the engine. Gus turned to her mother, stunned by the headlights' intensity.

They heard the crunch of footsteps on the gravel drive. They both peered into the dark evening. The only other sound was the snapping of the bug zapper hanging off the side of the caravan, as it caught and sizzled its victims. The footsteps approached steadily.

Soon the outline of Sergeant Peters appeared, materialising like a spectre from the dark evening. The police officer wore his uniform and a grim look on his face.

Her mother rose from the caravan step, a flurry of concern and limbs in the dark. 'Terry? Is everything all right?'

She knew what her mother was thinking: *Alice*. Gus knew because she was thinking the same thing.

'Is it my daughter?' her mother asked, her voice quiet with terror.

'No,' Terry said. 'It's — there's been a call from a concerned member of the public.'

'About what?'

The police officer cleared his throat. 'About you, Delphine.'

'Me?' Her mother's hand fluttered to her heart.

'Yes,' Sergeant Peters replied. 'We'd just like to discuss with you your movements over the past few months.' He cleared his throat. 'There's also the matter of the Starlight till not balancing, as raised by your, er, employer.' He glanced at Gus, looking pained. 'Delphine, I have to ask you some questions.'

Chapter 27

Unable to sleep, Gus prowled the projection room. The clock on the wall said it was three am.

Before her mother had gone in the car with Sergeant Peters, Mrs Able had instructed Gus to watch over Artie and get him ready for school if she wasn't back in time.

From up there, Gus could see their caravan and keep an eye on Artie's comings and goings. She would make him pancakes for breakfast, she decided.

She hoped her mother was all right down at the station. Gus hadn't been able to get Deirdre's threats out of her mind. Nor could she shake the image of a figure emerging from the canefield, when the paddock was on fire, from her mind. She was convinced it was Troy, come to report them, claim his stolen property and worse. It was like the past was closing in on them. Her chest ached suddenly.

We were happy here, for a moment, Gus thought. Her mother had seemed lighter somehow. She had dressed in breezy clothes and worn her hair loose. She had smiled more. There had been no visitors squashed around the table in the caravan demanding readings, nor any desperate haggard faces handing over cash, meagre payment for looking into their dead's murky whereabouts. Their mother hadn't retreated to the caravan alone to rest or missed any family dinners at all. And no Troy coming to take his cut. No hurried exile from yet another temporary home.

And Gus hadn't made any lists to squash the rising panic, she realised. She hadn't needed to.

They had been there for nearly five weeks. And she loved it: the warm sun, the bright light, the fug caused by co-sleeping in the caravan. Yes, there had been the scare of the cane fire and the explosion in science class, as well as the prophecy of their impending doom made by both Frank's dad and comet guy at the store, but there had been so much more.

For one there been the promise of friends. Gus hoped she and Nicole could remain science partners, despite the awkward presentation in class. And there had been the prospect of finally belonging somewhere. Deirdre had been right. Gus had wanted that. Until last night, it seemed they might finally be able to call this place home. Perhaps in time Alice too would return to herself and them.

But now, it was ruined. Troy *must* have shown up. Gus knew you only had to scratch around the top layer of dirt in her mother's past to unearth worms and scraps of bone. She had effectively taken a car, even though it was to escape a bad situation. According to Troy, their mum also owed him money. And if Troy hadn't tracked them down, then Deirdre had committed to ruining them at the last screening. Right now, Sergeant Peters would be investigating just that.

Gus felt heavy with the knowledge they would have to move on again, and soon. And where would they go? Troy would take back his car and she was pretty sure they hadn't made enough yet to buy another. Besides, they were running out of places to go. They were running out of north.

She took a breath and looked skywards. Gus could see the stars, their glinting edges sharpened by the inkiness of the sky. There were so many of them, just like the so many places she had been that had never been home. Though they were beautiful, they made her feel lonely all of a sudden. She wished Henry would turn up and berate her for trespassing or something.

Gus turned the projector on, just to feel its calming warmth under her hands. She wondered what time it was and what exactly Sergeant Peters was asking her mother right now.

The clock on the wall now said three thirty am. It was officially Wednesday. She needed to choose the movie and place the ad in the local paper. The show must go on, she told herself. It would keep her mind busy. She thought of the manual she had stashed carefully under the double bed in the caravan. Maybe there was inspiration to be found in there. She wished she had brought it with her.

She had no idea what to choose, though she rifled through every shelf and box of canisters. The topical theme had worked last time, she told herself, when she had screened *Ghostbusters*. Now she needed a movie about cosmic themes. And miracles maybe.

As though guided by spirits at a Ouija table, her hands lit on a film tin. She looked around for Henry, but there was no one else with her in the projection room. She turned the canister over and read the title of the movie. It promised to be about space and other unknowns.

ET, it said.

ET — The Extra-Terrestrial.

Chapter 28

Two days later they came over the hill and down the drive dressed like characters from the film.

Grown adults were dressed like the children in the movie, the girl character in a striped shirt and dark overalls, the boy in a red hoodie and jeans.

They came dressed in sheets like Halloween ghosts and on pushbikes with plush aliens in their baskets.

They advanced like an army of extra-terrestrials on the drive-in grounds and took their spots, setting up camp chairs and blankets and picnics. They adjusted their speakers and tuned into the radio frequency for the film expectantly. Their chatter thrummed with anticipation. It seemed the only people who hadn't shown up from Calvary were Sergeant Peters and his mother.

It was June, Gus realised, and there was only one week to go until the comet was due to show up in their patch of sky. She had timed her programming well.

Today was also her birthday. In a weird sort of way, she felt they were all there for her. The moviegoers and the ghost and the impending doomsday comet were all celebrating with her, even if they didn't know it.

In the cafe their mother was flipping space burgers — a regular hamburger assembled in the shape of a flying saucer — while Artie was busy serving up purple moon cakes, which did indeed look craterous and tasted like rocks, despite being garnished with Smarties.

Gus had longed to talk about her mother's visit to the police station and what it meant for them. But her mother had remained tight-lipped, looking pale for the rest of the week. There had been no Team Able meeting tonight. Gus knew their time as caretakers of the Starlight would be coming to an end soon. The knowledge was a weight on her chest. It actually hurt to breathe when she thought about the fact they'd have to leave.

Still, she was determined to see this screening out. She hoped against hope that somehow, having the most successful screening at the Starlight yet would save them

their food orders — her mother's cooking — in genuine anticipation.

Gus's heart was like a panicked bird, crashing against her ribcage. She wished so hard Henry would appear. Or that Stevie would come and help her solve the disastrous problem of not having a film to screen when every car space was occupied.

As she peered out the window Gus saw a figure coming towards them across the burned field. For a moment her heart stopped. Was it Henry, come to save the day? No, it couldn't be, the figure didn't have his tummy. Was it Alice then, returning home early from her time at Gran's? But the figure was too tall to be Alice. Perhaps it was Stevie, returned finally to explain what his gravitational pull on her sister had been?

The figure continued towards them like something from a bad dream. Gus couldn't make out its face and as they got closer she saw it was dressed entirely in white, a spectral figure wafting over the fields, like a ghost come for them. Or an alien.

At one minute past seven the crowd stirred.

At the sound of their impatient coughing Gus tore her eyes from the spectre in the paddock and looked out at the crowd below. People were fidgeting in their seats and turning to look up at the projection room, their eyes impatient, and accusing. She recalled Henry's claim he had never started a movie late. Well, where was he when she needed his impeccable punctuality?

Gus shrunk back in the room until she was out of sight. Blood rushed in her ears. She had to solve this. But how? She counted slowly to calm herself, naming the titles of the films she had screened, the way Gran had taught her. She tried to block out the low angry hum of the crowd below. But it didn't help. Counting the films only reminded her of the ticking clock, the minutes she had left to find a film to screen before the night was scheduled to begin.

She looked at the projector for inspiration, but it was silent, the power light blinking, almost taunting her to get started. She could hear her mother and Artie issuing free snacks and drinks, trying to placate the crowd below. There was a clang of plastic on metal. Someone had thrown something at the screen. Gus wanted to scream, hide and cry, all at the same time.

She heard a knock on the door of the projection room.

Thank goodness, she thought.

But when Gus opened the door, it was not Henry or Stevie but someone in a Halloween costume who stood there. Someone in a sheet dressed up as a ghost, complete with holes cut out for their eyes, entered the room. There was something familiar about the cold blue irises that gazed back at her.

Gus gasped and stepped back in shock. The ghost took another step towards her. When it spoke, there was something familiar about its voice.

'I thought I *warned* you, Gus Able,' the ghost said.

'I, u-uh—' Gus stammered, her heart in her throat. 'Who are you? And what did you warn me about, exactly?'

But the ghost did not reply. It took another step towards her, nearly tripping on the hem of the sheet.

'Dammit,' said the ghost, throwing off the white material in frustration.

There stood Deirdre, hair askew. She was without lipstick and wore regular clothes, shorts and a faded T-shirt.

Gus gasped in shock. 'Miss Cronk?' she exclaimed. 'Are you *dead*?'

'How *dare* you say that to a woman without her makeup on? You think you're *sooo* clever, *don't* you?' Deirdre replied.

It appeared she was not dead. Deirdre continued before Gus could think of a reply.

'I concede you *might* have a talent for picking movies. But if you're so *smart*, why didn't you quit after the *last* time I came around to warn you?'

Gus wasn't sure why she hadn't quit now either, come to think of it. Deirdre took in the empty cabinets and smiled smugly. 'Not so smart *now*, are we? Well, if you know what's *good* for you and your family, you'll stop trying to prove you're raising this place from the *dead*. Because,' Deirdre said, leaning in, 'I'm smart *too*, Augusta Able. I knew as soon as I saw you all rock up in that cereal box of a *car* that you were desperately concealing something. I've done my *homework*. I know what your mother *is*: *a common thief.*'

Gus felt a curl of fear in her gut. Had it been Deirdre, not Troy, who had alerted Sergeant Peters to their past? There wasn't time to enquire. Deirdre barrelled on.

'I *also* know what your mother used to do for a *living*. All that *wu-wu* nonsense.'

She circled her hands theatrically around her head. Gus swallowed. The secret they had tried so hard to hide was out.

'Is that so, Miss Cronk?' came a voice from the doorway.

Both Gus and Deirdre whirled to face them.

'What's going on here?' asked Mrs Able, concern in her voice. 'Gus, are you OK?'

'*Hello*, Delphine,' Deirdre said in a fake voice. 'I see, you've *finally* prised yourself away from your greasy *frypan*. As I was *just* saying to Augusta, I have become aware of your former *enterprise* and your dubious *associates*. I may have even let the local *authorities* know.'

'I see,' said Mrs Able.

'So, unless you want your secret *exposed* to these cosmically deluded *locals*, you'll *give up* on your little dream of building an entertainment *empire*. You don't want *that*, do you?'

'Deirdre, before you threaten us—' Mrs Able began.

'No,' Gus cut in. 'We don't. We don't want that, Mum.'

Who knew how the locals would react? She didn't want her mother to be harangued again by requests for readings or to disappear in a fog of sadness again. She knew her brother and sister didn't want that either. Her mother's gift may even be misunderstood and they could be driven out of town. It had certainly happened to Gran before. Gus wanted to stay there, more than anything.

'There is only room for *one* patron of the *arts* in this town, and that is me,' Deirdre was saying. 'I *did* warn you once *before*, Augusta. And if you want to keep a roof over your head for your *children* even for tonight, you'll concede *defeat*, Delphine. Because after this —' she gestured out at the cranky crowd, and then back at the empty projector '— you certainly won't be staying in Calvary.'

Gus's mother's face resembled a crushed shirt.

It seemed either way they were going to lose to the monster. In the stories Gus read, the good guys prevailed, eventually. But this wasn't a story. It was real life.

'Well?' Deirdre demanded.

Mrs Able nodded yes, sadly.

'*Right*, now that's settled, you are going to go out and tell the *locals* that the movie is off,' Deirdre instructed. 'Explain you've no *film* to screen. You'll take the *blame*, of course. And then they'll be all *dressed up* with nowhere to *go*.'

She paused and then smiled, rather like a cat might advancing on a mouse. 'Unless of *course*, they come to the *theatre*.'

'It's the last week of *Les Misérables*,' Gus guessed.

'*Exactly*. I'm glad we *understand* each other. And while you're *at* it, hand out these two-for-one passes to my show, *won't* you?' Deirdre demanded, producing a stack of tickets.

She waved them at mother and daughter.

'OK,' said Mrs Able, sounding defeated. 'But before we do, can you tell me one thing?'

'*Fine*,' said Deirdre. 'It's your *funeral*.'

'Why are you doing this? Why employ me as the caretaker and pressure us to sell tickets when you had no intention of reviving the drive-in?'

Deirdre regarded Gus and her mother, her head tilted to one side, thoughtfully. 'I didn't think you'd actually *achieve* anything,' the Director of the local Amateur Dramatic Society admitted. 'Granted, I asked you to keep the place *ticking over* while I sorted out the *administrative issues* around my father's estate. In fact, my solicitor has said I should have a response from the court *very soon*. I *admit* the extra cash you've brought in has allowed me to *up the ante* with my *production* values. But I did not expect such *insolence* — *arrogance* even — to think you could *succeed* where others have *failed*. It's the only time I've been *wrong* about you.'

Chapter 29

'Gus? Gus, wake up, darling.'

Gus opened her eyes in the midnight caravan. She made out her mother's face hovering above her, moon-white in the darkness. Mrs Able held the small torch she used for reading. She was in her summer nightie, a cardigan pulled close around her.

'Let's go outside,' her mother said gently. 'It's time we had a talk.'

Gus looked at the sleeping Artie, her mind still waking up.

'He'll be OK,' Delphine said, reading Gus's mind. 'He's out to it. Big night,' her mother said, a regretful tone to her voice.

Earlier, Gus had tossed and turned for ages, unable to sleep with the weight of her failure pressing all around her.

She'd been the one to 'fess up. She'd turned the projector off and walked down the steps with her shocked mother, while Deirdre watched from the projection room window. Gus had summoned Artie and the three of them had moved from group to group handing out refunds and takeaway meals explaining the sad state of affairs, that there would be no movie tonight. The crowd had expressed all stages of grief collectively: first denial, then anger. They had bargained with Gus through mouthfuls of dinner, got teary and then finally, they had accepted the bad news, drifting off in their costumes towards their cars, pocketing their refunds.

Her mother's eyes were still sad.

'It's time we had a talk,' Mrs Able said again to Gus. 'We're long overdue.'

She extended a hand to Gus and Gus rose with effort from the bed, trying not to wake Artie. She felt as though she weighed about the same as a comet.

They sat on the caravan steps once more. The night was cool, winter had arrived on cue. Gus shrank into her pyjamas. She waited for her mother to speak, dread pooling in her belly. She hadn't had dinner, she realised. She hadn't been hungry after Deirdre's visit and the humiliation of having to tell everyone the bad news.

Some twelfth birthday this had turned out to be.

She wondered what her mother was going to say. Gus already had a pretty good idea: they would have to leave again. And it was Gus's fault this time, though her mother wouldn't say so. She wished she had listened to Deirdre's threats the first time.

Her mother was quiet for a time and, unable to stand it, Gus spoke. 'I'm sorry I didn't tell you Deirdre warned me earlier, Mum,' she said.

She paused. Her mother didn't say anything, so Gus continued, her voice low. 'It's my fault this has happened. And now she knows about you. About what you do. What you *did*,' Gus corrected herself.

Her mother nodded. 'Yes,' she said looking at the sky. 'That's what Sergeant Peters wanted to talk to me about.'

Gus's eyes filled with tears. She knew it. They were leaving this place.

'That isn't what I want to talk to you about though, Gus,' her mother said.

'It isn't?' Gus replied. She thought it was really something they *ought* to talk about.

'There's nothing to worry about on that front. Not now, anyway. It's true, Deirdre *did* look me up online.' Her mother paused as though debating whether to go on. Gus looked at her expectantly and Mrs Able continued. 'Turns out when we were still living with him Troy advertised my services as a psychic on a few dodgy trading post-type sites, without my knowledge, of course. Deirdre called the number listed and got Troy. She confirmed our description and the Camry's licence plate. Troy of course, told her all about my taking his car. And she went straight down to the Calvary Police Station.'

'Oh no,' said Gus.

'But it's all straightened out now,' her mother assured her. 'And there's no stealing charge for the Starlight either, because I showed him the books. Alice did such a good job balancing the ticket sales and Deirdre's precious float was all accounted for. Despite her ravings earlier tonight.'

'Oh,' said Gus, relieved. 'Thank goodness.'

'So now, I want to talk about you,' her mother said.

Mrs Able looked down at Gus, who was sagged on the second step. She seemed to not know what to say next. She deliberated, hesitation showing on her features, before plunging in. 'You may have noticed some, er, recent changes, Gus,' her mother began. She cleared her throat. 'With you. With ah, the onset of maturity.'

Wait, were they having *that* kind of talk? Gus wiped her eyes. She was grateful it was dark. Her mother wouldn't be able to see her face. Mrs Able continued.

'In our family, when an Able girl turns twelve, something er, surprising happens,' her mother said. 'And I fear it's been happening to you.'

Gus wanted to point out that it wasn't just the Able girls, it was *all* girls. So Ms McKenzie had said during PE class, anyway.

'Gus, are you listening to what I am saying?' her mother asked.

'Yes, Mum,' she managed.

'Well … is it happening to you?' her mother prompted, her voice strained.

'It's normal, Mum,' Gus mumbled back, embarrassed.

Her mother looked taken aback. Then she nodded. 'Perhaps it happens more than we know,' she acknowledged. She cleared her throat again. 'Anyway, I'm glad you're taking it so well,' Mrs Able said. 'When it first happened to me, I was terrified.'

Gus waited for her to continue. She didn't have words.

'All those desperate people, so searching and so sad.'

That's a bit dramatic, Gus thought.

She paused.

'And so, well, *dead*.'

'Wait, what?' Gus cut in.

It did not appear as though they were on the same wavelength. Were they talking about the same thing?

'I wouldn't be surprised if you're feeling anxious or glum,' her mother continued.

'We're not talking about hormones, Mum?'

'No, Gus,' said Mrs Able seriously. 'I'm talking about *seeing ghosts*. The rite of passage for every Able woman when she turns twelve.'

'Oh *that*,' Gus said, relieved. 'Yeah, I've been seeing dead people for like, months, Mum.'

'Really?' replied her mother. 'I mean, I suspected last week, but there's been so much going on lately, what with Alice and the police becoming involved ...' She paused. 'Wait, what do you mean months? Your birthday is today.'

'I've been seeing ghosts since we got here,' Gus said recalling her first encounter with Henry.

'You have?'

Gus nodded. Maybe even before that, she thought. She recalled the pale woman that night at the service station.

'You always hit your milestones early, Gus,' her mother said proudly. Then she turned serious, her thoughts coming out in a jumble. 'But are you OK? Were you scared? Oh, I'm so sorry I didn't notice,' her mother fretted.

'It was scary at first,' Gus admitted. 'But then lately it hasn't been so bad. And now I feel like that's the least of our problems, you know? What with the doomsday comet coming, and running the drive-in.'

Her mother nodded again slowly. 'I must admit you're taking it better than Alice did.'

'Wait, Alice can see ghosts, too?' Gus asked.

'That's what I'm saying, darling,' her mother replied. 'It's something all the Able women inherit. Like a gift. Or a curse,' she sighed. 'At least it feels that way until you learn to manage it.'

Gus's mind was racing. She had thought the gift/curse hadn't touched her sister because she hadn't mentioned anything. But then so much had been up with Alice lately, since before they'd even arrived here. She recalled the scene at school when the boys were calling her sister weird, and the moment at the drive-in when Stevie had said Alice was different from other girls. She had thought Stevie was in love with Alice, and maybe he was, but maybe he also meant this. Alice must have told him about it and somehow the other kids at school found out. No wonder she had been so upset with Stevie at the store.

It was all starting to make sense. Gus realised it wasn't only her mum who had been recently outed as a medium, but potentially Alice too, putting their family doubly at risk. She'd have to keep quiet about her own extra-celestial ability. At least Artie was safe, being a boy.

'Mum, what are we going to do?' Gus asked.

'I don't actually know,' her mother said honestly. 'When we arrived here, I felt so sure this was the place we were meant to be. It's hard to accept I was wrong. But,' she added, 'whatever we do next or wherever we go, I promise we'll do it together.'

'What do you mean, Mum?' Gus thought they already had.

Mrs Able took a deep breath. 'I know I haven't always been the most … present … mother at times,' she began. 'Sometimes, in the past I was too, too —' she searched for the right word '— *sad* to see what was in front of me. To see how wonderful you all are. Maybe I haven't said that enough. Maybe I haven't told you how smart and lovely and funny and brave you've been.'

Her mother took another deep breath. There were fireworks in Gus's heart.

'But now, with the ghosts and the Troys out of the way, I can see it all more clearly. You are a wonder, Gus.' Mrs Able put her arm around her middle daughter and kissed the top of her head.

'Thanks, Mum,' Gus said. 'You're pretty amazing too.'

Her mother smiled. 'Stay here,' said Mrs Able. 'I'll be right back.'

She stood up and went inside the caravan.

Gus contemplated the stars. She had to find a way to fix this, though right now she had no idea how.

When her mother returned, she was carrying a chocolate cake with pink icing and twelve candles. She produced a box of matches and lit the candles, one by one, until they twinkled brighter than the stars.

'Happy birthday, darling,' her mother whispered.

Chapter 30

A couple of days later, Gus was again woken in the early morning by the flicker of fire on the caravan wall. Another cane fire, she assumed, rolling over to catch a bit more sleep before it was time to get up for school.

Thankfully they'd had a quiet weekend. They had spoken to Alice on the phone last night. Her sister had dutifully answered their mother's questions. Yes, she had been brushing her teeth. Yes, she had been doing the English lessons set by her teacher. No, she hadn't been chased by any spirits at Gran's. The farm appeared ghoul-free, save for the ghost army of indignant roast chooks. She had become vegetarian, she said, after encountering these tiny, plucked spectres. Also, she was ready to come home soon.

Chapter 31

Deirdre's face was a triumphant sneer as she surveyed Gus, her mother and Artie, sitting on the caravan steps.

The Ables huddled together under a smoky blanket, clutching the cups of weak tea a kindly firefighter had made for them. Gus couldn't stop the tears leaking from her eyes although the Calvary Regional Fire Brigade had finally extinguished the blaze.

The sun was up, hovering over the now-singed drive-in sign. Everything was coloured burnt orange, even the morning sky.

The Director of the local Amateur Dramatic Society stood in the middle of the drive-in wearing a ruby-red dressing gown, soot smeared theatrically across her cheeks, surveying the ruins.

Firefighters were busy roping off the burned-out building.

The entire top storey of the building, the projection room, was destroyed, while the bottom part containing the cafe was a shell of blackened walls. The cooking equipment, the tables and all of their mother's inventory were burned to ash. The drive-in screen too had been almost consumed by the blaze. Only the poles supporting it remained.

The caravan, the toilet block and the Starlight sign were the only things that had escaped the reach of the fire. The latter was spared due to the quick action of the fire brigade.

Sergeant Peters was inside the caravan, interviewing witnesses with the door closed. These were a cane farmer who had come to check his pre-dawn field and an early-rising dog walker with a blue heeler. The dog crouched in the ash while its owner gave her account to the police officer about what she'd seen, the dog looking as dejected as Gus felt. From time to time the police officer glanced through the window in their direction. Gus knew it would be their turn soon.

Dread pooled in her gut like tar smoke. This was all her fault. What was going to happen to them now?

Would she be arrested? If Gus went to jail for burning down the place, what would become of her mother and her brother and sister? Her mother would have to take on extra spirit readings to pay for Gus's consumables in jail: toothpaste and reading materials and fruit so she wouldn't get scurvy.

She glanced at her mum, who sat looking defeated on the front step of the caravan, one arm around Artie. She too had tears in her eyes, which made Gus feel even worse than the dog cringing in the ashes. She wanted to say she hadn't meant to burn their home and their business down, but her throat was scorched and the words were like lumps of coal.

The caravan door opened and the cane farmer and dog walker filed silently past the family on the steps. The woman retrieved her dog and they all left through the haze. The police sergeant, finished with the other witnesses, appeared in the caravan doorway.

Deirdre, seeing his intention, made a beeline for the Ables too, like an ibis who has spotted an overflowing rubbish bin.

Sergeant Peters crouched to Gus's level. She wanted to close her eyes and disappear or run away. All of a sudden, she understood her mother's instinct to flee.

'I think I've got the picture regarding what's happened here,' Sergeant Peters said. 'But I still need to ask you a few questions, Gus,' he added, not unkindly. 'Is that all right with you?'

'*I'd* very much like to ask a question or two *myself*,' Deirdre interjected. 'At the *top* of my list is: what the *hell* were you thinking, *girl*?'

'Miss Cronk,' the police officer cautioned. 'This is a police matter for investigation.'

'An investigation on *my* property,' the Director of the local Amateur Dramatic Society countered. 'Involving *my* commercial business.'

That isn't technically correct, Gus thought. But she knew she wasn't in a position to argue right now.

'That may be, Miss Cronk, though I think you'll find you have only one legal employee on the books, unless you have been profiteering from child labour?' the police officer replied.

'I, er, certainly not,' Deirdre huffed.

'Right then, for the time being, I ask that you avoid speculation until the cause of the event is fully determined and the appropriate next steps are taken,' Sergeant Peters cautioned.

'*Speculation*? Fully *determined*? Appropriate next

steps?' Deirdre spluttered. 'They've burned down my *property*! Razed it to the *ground*. The appropriate *next steps* are eviction, recompense, or failing that, *jail*!'

There were the words Gus was most afraid of. 'Please don't make us leave,' she whispered.

'You'll do more than *that*!' Deirdre spat. 'You'll disappear, you little *vandal*! Vamoose! Evaporate. You and your no-good *family*. I regret *ever* employing you.'

'Stop it right there, Miss Cronk,' the sergeant intervened. 'Or I'll write you up for harassment.'

'*Harassment*! You can't be *serious*, Terry. *I* am the wronged party here. And I'll see that they *pay* for this.'

'Miss Cronk, please,' Mrs Able interjected. 'Gus didn't mean to—'

But Deirdre ignored her mother, speaking right over the top of her. 'Carmichael,' she shouted. 'Mayne!'

The two men Gus had seen once before prowling about the drive-in with Deirdre emerged out of the ashes. Like vultures, Gus thought. Again, both wore spectacles, while one wore a brown suit, and the other a blue one.

'Yes, Miss Cronk?' they replied, their voices oily.

'As you can *see*, gentlemen, my father's assets — my *inheritance* — have been severely *compromised*.'

Deirdre glared at Gus again. 'A new valuation is required at *once*, Carmichael,' she continued, clicking her fingers.

The real estate agent snapped to attention, pulling a phone from his pocket in preparation to take photos.

'And potentially *damages*,' she added, clicking her fingers at Mayne.

The lawyer nodded vigorously and pulled out a notebook and pen from his shiny leather briefcase. The three moved in the direction of the Moonbeam, or the former site of the cafe, anyway.

'Right, back to my questions ...' Sergeant Peters said, looking annoyed.

Gus barely registered what the police officer was saying. She couldn't take her eyes off Deirdre and her two advisers, who were measuring and appraising the drive-in site until Gus feared their eyes might roll out of their heads. She felt a burning sensation in her stomach, which she was surprised to recognise as anger. It was left to Gus's mother to answer the police officer's questions while Gus drifted closer to the three to eavesdrop. She overheard Sergeant Peters enquiring if the projector had been left on as she headed for the toilet block, which stood between the caravan and

262

the site of the former cafe. She lingered by the wall out of sight.

'I must say, Deirdre, you've come out on top, here,' she heard Mayne say. 'Even despite your application to have your father declared dead being denied.'

'This place has actually increased in value now that those scruffy old buildings are gone,' Carmichael enthused. 'As I said before, on the highway like this, it's prime real estate.'

'They've done you a favour, that family,' Mayne sniffed. 'It will make the transfer of the estate more straightforward when the time comes, now your father's wishes for it to remain a drive-in have been rendered void, due to the fire.'

'There *is* a silver lining *after all*,' Deirdre said, a smile in her voice. 'And if there *isn't*,' she added, 'you've got to make one *yourself*.'

Something about the way she said it made Gus's ears prick up.

'Deirdre, you old fox. Are you saying you had a hand in this fire business?' chortled Carmichael.

'Now, now, no leading the witness,' joked Mayne.

What exactly were they saying? That Deirdre had caused the fire? That it hadn't been Gus's fault after all?

'When the court didn't fast-track my father's death certificate, I was *compelled* to act, you'll both agree. *Sometimes* one has to take one's destiny in one's *own* hands.'

Before she knew it, Gus had emerged from where she had been hiding. 'You did this,' she said loud enough for everyone to hear.

Her mother, Artie and Sergeant Peters all looked at her, their conversation halted mid-discussion.

It was as though some voice outside Gus had said the words, some braver, stronger version of herself.

Deirdre and her entourage turned and regarded her too.

'I beg your pardon?' Deirdre replied, her eyes aflame.

'It was you who started the fire in the projection room,' Gus repeated, slowly walking towards the three. 'I didn't leave the projector on. I remember now. I remember switching it off after *ET* was cancelled.'

'That is *absurd*,' said Deirdre. 'Simply *preposterous*.'

Gus continued as though Deirdre hadn't spoken. 'I didn't leave the film in the projector either.' Gus paused. 'I couldn't have. Because you took all the films, didn't you? Before the weekend!'

Deirdre's red lips formed an 'o' shape. 'This is *outrageous*,' she spluttered. 'It's not enough that you *destroy* my property. Now you have to accuse *me* of setting fire to it?'

'What's going on there?' Sergeant Peters called.

The lawyer, the real estate agent and Deirdre moved towards Gus, closing in and surrounding her. Gus swallowed. Mrs Able stood on the step. The police officer began to walk to where Gus and the co-conspirators stood.

'You'll *pay* for this, Gus Able,' Deirdre said in a low voice. Gone was the modulated trill, in its place was a voice as hard as steel. 'You'll get what you *deserve*,' she added. 'I *told* you there can only be one patron of the arts in *this* town!'

The trio nodded and closed in even more tightly around Gus.

'Give her some space,' the police officer ordered.

Gus was relieved he had reached her side. Out of the corner of her eye she saw her mother hurrying over too, Artie in tow.

And *Henry*! Materialising through the smoke haze, as though he were a hero from an old war movie, albeit a hero in a terry-towelling fishing hat, the projectionist stalked determinedly up the Starlight drive on his bandy legs.

Everyone stopped still. The blood drained from Deirdre's face. 'Dad?' she said, choking on the last *d*. 'Is it really *you*?'

'Indeed, it is, daughter, and good morning to you,' Henry said. Henry nodded to the assembled group. He tipped his fishing hat to Terry.

'Morning, folks. Hello, Sergeant Peters,'

'Henry?' Sergeant Peters exclaimed. 'Er, hello.'

'Dad?' Deirdre said, again. 'But I — I thought ...'

Gus watched with interest. It appeared she hadn't encountered her father yet, post-death. Her accomplices gaped. Mrs Able and Sergeant Peters too seemed stupefied by Henry's appearance.

'What's the matter, Deirdre darling, cat got your tongue? Don't you have a hug for your old dad?'

'Yes, yes, of *c-course*,' Deirdre stammered, moving closer, though she still appeared reluctant to touch him.

'Come here, Dee Dee,' Henry said, pulling his daughter in for a bear hug. 'You look peaky, love. As though you've seen a ghost.'

'Oh!' Deirdre said, as she was enveloped in Henry's

arms, clearly alarmed. 'It's really *you*. I can't *believe* it. I thought … I thought you had d-d-d—'

'Shush now, I'm here, darling,' Henry soothed. He pulled his daughter closer, if it were possible.

It was a very real scene, for a ghost. Henry seemed to be squeezing his daughter with real arms with real ginger hair on them. He appeared to have real sunburn on his face, perhaps from living in the hut by the river.

'What's going on here, anyway?' Henry asked, releasing Deirdre.

'Oh *Dad*,' Deirdre, said, tearing up suddenly. 'They've burned down the *drive-in*. The Starlight. Everything you've *built*. Everything you've created is *gone*.'

'I can see that,' Henry said. 'It's a crying shame.'

'It's all *their* fault,' Deirdre said. 'Those people. Those … psychics!' She pointed an accusing finger at Gus and her mother.

'Is that true, Sergeant Peters?' Henry asked.

'That matter is still under investigation,' the police officer replied, having found his voice again.

Henry nodded.

'They'll have to *leave*, of course,' Deirdre said, her voice dripping with vitriol.

'Oh, I don't know about that,' said Henry, mildly.

'What do you *mean*?' Deirdre replied, stepping back from her father.

'Just what I say, love. It's not your drive-in, it's mine. So I decide what to do with it. Who stays and who goes. Psychic medium or otherwise.'

'But, but,' Deirdre spluttered.

Wait, what? Gus thought. Was Henry saying —?

'You're not dead?' Gus blurted out. 'You're not a ghost, after all?'

Henry looked offended. 'I know I am not the most youthful-looking bloke at the drive-in presently, but no, Gus, I'm not dead yet, as far as I can tell.'

'B-but I thought …' Gus stammered.

Everyone was gaping at them: Mrs Able, Sergeant Peters, Deirdre and her henchmen.

She took a breath and tried again to make sense of things. 'Deirdre said, when we first arrived, you'd gone missing. You'd taken one last long walk to the river to fish. She … she said you were … dearly departed, gone on to that great movie theatre in the sky.'

'Did she now?' Henry replied, one eyebrow raised at his daughter.

The Director of the local Amateur Dramatic Society scowled at Gus.

268

'Perhaps that's what she wished for,' Henry said, 'however I can assure you all that I am standing here as flesh and blood.'

'I can corroborate that,' Sergeant Peters said.

'Thank you for your valiant efforts and your discretion, Sergeant, in the matter of my er, disappearance,' Henry said.

'*Wait* a minute,' Deirdre said, wheeling on the police officer. 'Do you mean to tell me that you *knew* my father was alive and didn't *tell* me? That you … you, *covered* for him, in some sort of ridiculous *caper*?'

'Sergeant Peters will neither confirm nor deny such accusations,' said Henry. 'He is not the guilty party here.' He looked at the group in turn to explain. 'I've been holed up in my fishing hut. Apart from a few visits I made to check on the wellbeing of the Starlight.' Henry winked at Gus, then continued. 'I just needed some time away, to think and decide what I want for the place. In perpetuity.'

He looked over at his daughter and added loudly in a clear voice, 'I won't sign your Power of Attorney, darling. And as the owner of the Starlight I say what happens to it, as well as who stays and who goes.'

Chapter 32

That evening, as Gus swept ash from the scorched concrete floor of the Moonbeam Cafe, she reflected on the day's events.

Her back ached and her clothes, face and hands were covered in soot. Artie joked she looked like Cinderella. They were all exhausted and had barely stopped for lunch. The Ables had been cleaning up all day.

It's so funny the way things turn out, Gus thought. Yesterday she had been so afraid they would have to leave this place and now they had Henry's blessing to stay. But what were they going to do there? Thanks to the fire, they were now unemployed. Without a cafe or a screen or a projection room there was no Starlight, and as far as Gus knew there were no further prospects for them in this town.

Gus's one comfort was that Sergeant Peters had directed Deirdre to join him down at the station for further questioning. Her mother, shocked and tearful, had invited Terry for dinner that evening. He accepted gratefully, then told her he would bring fish and chips from Calvary Takeaway, since they no longer had a proper kitchen and were limited by the tiny kitchenette in the caravan.

Her mother and Artie had gone into town to meet the bus. Gran had texted yesterday. Alice was coming home this evening.

Alice would probably be upset and disoriented when she saw the state of the place, Gus thought. It wouldn't be the perfect homecoming at all. Thankfully the caravan was still intact and Gus had to admit she looked forward to being lodged like a sardine in a tin tonight, mashed between her two siblings in the double bed. It was with surprise that she realised she had missed Alice, even the mostly silent Alice of recent months. Their family had felt wonky and off-kilter without her, like a car missing a fourth wheel.

Thank goodness for Henry, she reflected. He'd said they could stay until their mother found another job. Without him they'd be homeless right now. They'd be sleeping in the car tonight, probably in a back lot or by the side of the road somewhere. In that respect, the caravan was a step up, almost luxurious by comparison. Though she was still coming to terms with the fact Henry wasn't a ghost. It made her think she'd been wrong about the woman at the servo when they'd travelled here as well.

Gus felt disappointed that she hadn't inherited the gift of seeing the dead after all. Instead, Alice had. Alice had always been the special one, the talented and beautiful sister people were drawn to like moths to a flame. Even the wrong types of people. Much like their mother had been, Gus thought. She recalled the sad and nasty words spoken in their lounge rooms in their houses in various outer suburbs of their last city, the grey faces around the small table.

Gus told herself she had dodged a curse. Alice had seemed very troubled lately and this explained it. She hoped her sister would be OK. In time, perhaps she would learn to deal with seeing ghosts and perhaps even help them, the way their mother had.

Poor Alice. First the curse of seeing dead people and then the curse of falling in love. For that had been what had happened to Alice and Stevie, Gus felt sure.

Talk about double whammy puberty, seeing ghosts *and* having hormones. Teenage love seemed totally gross, Gus concluded. She could live without it.

As Gus gathered the ash she had swept up in a dustpan, the bulbs powering the drive-in sign hissed and snapped. Bugs danced around the light, probably convinced it was the moon. Apart from the glow from the sign the evening was dark, the stars not yet out.

Gus remembered what Ms McKenzie had said, the comet was due across their patch of sky soon, the coming weekend, in fact. What would it look like? Would it be a smattering of dust and gas like Nicole had said? Or beautiful slipstreams of light, a romantic show in the sky the way their teacher described? Or were the locals in fact correct? Would it be an annihilating celestial body, exploding as it hit earth's atmosphere, shattering into a million projectile-like pieces? Could they watch it and ooh and aah, or would they have to wear protective glasses and safety boots? Would they have to shelter from its wrath and radioactive glow? Tonight the sky seemed so benign, like a warm dark embrace, the kind you get before you sink into sleep.

Gus remembered something her gran liked to say, it was always darkest before the dawn.

It did indeed seem dire for their family right now, no work, no money, no prospects. What on earth were the Able family going to do?

Gus leaned on the broom in the shell of the former cafe and watched a star peep through the dark curtain of the sky. It seemed the only thing that the drive-in was good for now was star gazing. The burned-out paddock and now the mostly destroyed screen gave them an uninterrupted view of the evening sky.

It's an expanse of promise, Gus thought suddenly.

They'd have a great view come Saturday night, which Ms McKenzie had said was expected to have ideal conditions to see the comet.

Nearly falling off her broom, Gus craned her neck to take in the vastness of the night sky. It just might work, she told herself ... it was only Tuesday, so she still had time to advertise in the local newspaper ...

She heard the sky-blue car roll up the drive. She would need her family's help, she mused. She couldn't possibly pull it off on her own.

Chapter 33

Like the night Gus had planned to screen *ET*, again the locals came to the drive-in in droves.

It was as though word had got out about Deirdre's act of sabotage and people actually wanted to support the Ables. Not to mention buy a front-row seat at a cosmic miracle — or disaster depending on how you looked at it. They arrived in their beat-up cars, faces solemn. Even the faces of the little kids were serious, and the family pets looked grave too. In their car boots they had jammed end-of-days supplies: jerry-cans of water, cartons of tinned foods and blankets piled high.

They wore trackpants, stained work singlets and active wear, while the kids were in flannelette pyjamas. Gus supposed if the end really was nigh, it made sense to be comfortable while watching humanity being turned to powder.

They came as though this might be the last time. They came as though expecting a miracle.

This time, in the paper, Gus had simply advertised the event as an evening of comet spotting. Everyone had heard about the fire and the locals knew the Starlight had the most uninterrupted view of the night sky in these parts now there was no longer a screen cluttering the skyline.

Gus was banking everything on Riley's Comet appearing. She charged modest prices, advertised a family discount pass, and even offered a refund if the comet was a no-show. Henry had lent Mrs Able his barbecue and she and Artie were serving sausages in bread for a dollar a snag. The locals were eating them as fast as they could cook them.

It was coming up to six thirty pm, and according to the latest news predictions, the comet was expected to course through their patch of sky at around seven, when the darkness was rich and established, hanging around them like a cosy blanket.

Gus and her family had a prime viewing spot, the best seats in the house. After she had allocated all the customers a spot, she climbed onto the caravan roof with a tray of snacks. Nicole sat there already in one of the folding chairs Gus had arranged, sipping from a travel mug filled with green juice her mother had made.

'Nicole,' Gus said when she saw what her friend was drinking, 'tonight could well be the end of the world. Will you have a delicious cup of dairy and sugar whipped together with artificial flavours instead? Just this once? For me?'

Nicole regarded the strawberry milkshake Gus offered, which Terry had brought them all from town, with a horrified look on her face. 'All right,' she said, her features relaxing into a grin. 'Just don't tell my mum.'

Gus grinned back at her friend. Together they watched Gus's family take the punters' tickets and hand out complimentary water and snacks donated by a local business. Artie was dressed in a suit made of aluminium foil. He wore a hat he and Alice had made, featuring antennae of coat-hanger wire. Alice joked that he had a direct line to the comet tonight.

Her sister seemed better after her time away with Gran — more like her old self. She had attended school all week and reported on her studies around the dinner table. Not even the sight of the footy boys sitting front-row centre at the drive-in tonight, still wearing their muddy training gear and with Nathan at the helm, appeared to rattle her. Maybe she had just needed some time out.

Gus watched as Alice approached to check their tickets. Nathan rose and said something and the others cracked up laughing. Alice took a step back.

Gus stood on the roof of the caravan and, before she knew it, without a word to Nicole, she was climbing down and making her way quickly over to Alice and the boys.

'I heard the mother is a psychic,' Gus overheard one of them say.

'Like, someone who talks to dead people?' Nathan replied. 'Alice, if that's true, your family is more messed up than I thought!'

Gus stood beside her sister. She wanted to take Alice's hand, but she was afraid to in front of the footy boys.

'Oh look, it's the school psychic's little sister. Do you talk to dead people, too?' Nathan jeered.

Gus shrank a little beside Alice.

Her sister didn't reply. Instead she turned her head to one side. She gazed intently at a spot directly over Nathan's left shoulder. She watched the spot for a while, as though transfixed, and then blinked, as though whatever she had been looking at was now gone. It was impossible to miss and all the footy boys looked less amused now. In fact they looked a little puzzled. Maybe even a little worried.

'Pardon, what did you say?' Alice asked Nathan. 'I got distracted by something.'

'Um, what did you just see back there?' Nathan replied.

'Oh, nothing too bad,' Alice said. 'I don't expect they'll harm you.'

Alice then directed her gaze downwards, at Nathan's footy boots, where his laces were a tangle of spaghetti. 'Better watch those laces,' she said. 'You could trip and hurt yourself.'

Nathan opened his mouth and closed it again. All of the other footy boys seemed out of words too.

'Now, can I see your admission tickets?' Alice asked politely.

The boys meekly handed over their tickets to be checked one by one. Hands in their pockets, they sat back down in their spots. Gus felt stuck to the ground too. She couldn't believe what she had just seen, but she had loved every minute of the show.

'Coming, Gus?' asked Alice. She flipped her sheet of honey hair as she stalked off to the next group.

The footy boys looked after her, stupefied. Gus wanted to high-five her sister, but she thought that might break the spell. Gus followed Alice through the crowd, watching her work, wondering all the while what Gran had said to help her sister during their time together. Whatever wisdom Alice had gleaned during her time away, she was back on form now, a true celestial queen.

Gus returned to the caravan, climbed back onto the roof and settled back in her chair. She was unused to having nothing to do but wait. Tonight, she didn't have to find the movie, feed the spools, or remember to switch anything on or off. All she had to do was watch. And she planned to train her eyes on the sky like a laser beam so as not to miss any sign of the comet. She didn't want to miss a moment and she didn't want their movie patrons to, either. They couldn't afford the refunds.

Gus wondered how it would feel when the comet blitzed them, the way the online article on Nicole's laptop had claimed it would. Would the collision be quick, like the blink of an eye, or would she feel herself fragmenting into a million tiny pieces, as Riley's did its work?

She supposed she should be sad or at least afraid right now, but weirdly she felt almost happy. Her family were all together again and her best friend was by her side. Gus hadn't ever thought she would be able to say those words: best friend. But there was Nicole, right beside her, giggling at nothing due to the rapid absorption of the sugar into her bloodstream.

Wait, Gus thought. Nicole wasn't giggling at nothing — there was a guy below them, knocking on the door. He wore boots, a white boiler suit and a homemade space helmet that appeared to be fashioned from plastic wrap and papier-mache. Over this ensemble he wore a hand-lettered sign that read: *The end is nighe!! Herald the new dawn of Riley's.*

It was the sandwich board man, Joe, from outside the store. Nicole looked at Gus, unable to speak for spluttering. Tears were streaming down her cheeks.

'Excuse me,' sandwich board guy said, looking at them, a peeved expression on his face. 'Where can I drop this off?' He brandished a pin-striped suit.

Gus looked at him blankly.

'Your sign says you're a drive-in and drycleaners?' the man prompted.

He pointed to the Starlight sign, still glowing bright after all that had happened.

'*Oh*,' said Gus. 'You can leave it here, I guess.' Her entrepreneurial brain began whirring. 'I'll take care of it,' she added.

He threw the suit towards them and Gus caught it. Then the man tottered off to sit on the grass and mumble at the sky, presumably invoking the comet's arrival.

When the tickets had all been checked and all the sausages in bread served up, the rest of the Able family joined Nicole and Gus on the roof. They sat together in companionable silence save for the sound of Artie munching popcorn and Nicole slurping her milkshake.

Her mother smiled and winked at Gus over the others' heads. There were no ghosts to be seen tonight and Gus was relieved. Just before seven pm, Sergeant Peters joined them on the caravan roof, where her mother had a spare chair waiting. Artie climbed down from the caravan to keep Mrs Peters company in their usual spot below.

They didn't have to wait long. The arrival of Riley's Comet was heralded by a ball of white light appearing in the night sky, to the right of where the Starlight screen had loomed. The white-hot sphere of the nucleus was edged in a blue and lavender ring. It glowed there for a minute, transfixing them all.

Gus held her breath as she waited for the comet to indicate its direction, and veer suddenly towards them. Instead, it began to change shape, forming a teardrop, revealing the beginnings of a tail. It resembled the form of many types of life, first a goldfish, then an embryo like the ones Ms McKenzie had shown them in PE class.

It seemed the whole of the drive-in audience was holding its collective breath as they watched the comet travel across the mid-section of the night sky, heading right and out of town, a gaseous tail streaming behind it. The comet seemed to take its time. It appeared to like the attention, the feeling of being watched and adored.

Gus too held her breath and waited for particles to break off and head towards them, huge molten rocks of doom. She waited for any sign of death or destruction, or even just a shower of electrical sparks.

But the town of Calvary remained untouched, and those sitting on the roof of the caravan, in the most direct line of danger, remained safe.

Gus breathed a sigh of relief, and to her surprise, felt tears slipping down her cheeks. She was so happy all of a sudden. So happy to be there, to be alive, along with this strange sample of humanity. The crowd ooh-ed and aah-ed until the comet was almost out of sight and Gus realised she finally knew what it was to be a part of something.

Riley's Comet had all but disappeared when she heard a pinging sound, something hard against metal. She ducked instinctively, each of them on the roof did. Could it be comet debris? Perhaps they weren't out of the woods yet.

When there wasn't another ping for an interval and the coast seemed clear she looked up to see the culprit.

Joe, the man with the sandwich board, was pegging rocks at the drive-in sign. He had hit the metal post first, but with a second better-aimed shot had shattered one of the bulbs.

The crowd gasped and a few stood to get a better look. The man bent to pick up another stone.

'Hey,' Gus called, 'leave our sign alone.'

'Farce!' the man ranted. 'Travesty! Come back, comet!'

The crowd began to murmur their displeasure.

'Come back, comet,' the man shouted. 'You missed us! You forgot me!'

On the roof of the caravan, Sergeant Peters stood. 'I'll just go sort this out,' he said to their mother. 'Joe,' he called, 'settle down there, mate.'

Sergeant Peters climbed down from the roof while the man with the sandwich board continued to rant.

'Well done, Gus,' the police officer said, looking back up at her. 'That was spectacular.'

Gus beamed like a star was inside her. She couldn't help it.

Looking over at Joe, dancing with rage under the Starlight sign, Sergeant Peters said, 'Never a dull moment in this town.'

Nicole turned to Gus on the roof. 'It might be the sugar and artificial flavours talking,' she said, 'but if I were a judge for the state science competition, you'd definitely be taking home the Mega-scope.'

Chapter 34

Gus cleaned up the empty bottles and discarded ticket stubs after the drive-in crowd cleared out. Everyone had drifted off home, star-struck, touches of comet dust in their eyes. She was delirious with fatigue and victory when she saw him.

Stevie seemed even taller and thinner than usual, as though time had stretched him out even more, but perhaps it was just Gus's exhausted mind playing tricks. Though when she squinted again, she saw it was true, he was thin as ether, or a wisp of smoke, his form almost quavering in the night air.

She really needed to get some sleep, she told herself.

Stevie was talking to Alice. They stood in the dark between the posts of the burned-out movie screen. They were talking closely and Gus could see how much they meant to each other. She was happy they had found a moment to be together again.

She wondered what he wanted to say to Alice so badly and why he had come back. She hoped it wouldn't send Alice off the rails again.

Gus sneezed, breaking the spell. The pair looked over and it seemed that Alice was smiling in her direction. She beckoned to Gus with a curled finger. Incredulous, Gus stepped towards them.

'Good evening, Gus,' Stevie said.

'Er, hi,' Gus replied.

Where have you been? she wanted to say. So much has happened here without you.

'Stevie has something he wants to say to you,' Alice said.

Alice smiled encouragingly at Stevie, as if to say *Go on*, and then drifted off into the shadows.

'I, um, don't know where to begin,' said Stevie.

Gus had no idea where to start either. Should she apologise for getting upset at the store?

Stevie moved to take her hand. His grip was so light she couldn't actually feel it and yet she knew his hand was there, like something outside of regular touch. Gus tried to remember to breathe.

'I suppose I ought to say thank you,' Stevie said, looking into her eyes. His glistened.

'You're welcome,' Gus replied, in surprise. 'Um, for what, though?'

'For everything,' Stevie said throwing his arms open. 'For tonight and the comet. For introducing me to Alice.'

That was a bit like taking a hit from one of Artie's cap-gun bullets, Gus thought.

'For seeing me,' Stevie added quietly.

She was confused again. 'What do you mean?' Gus asked.

'I've been hanging around the Starlight for a long time, Gus,' Stevie said. 'A very long time. And you were the first to.'

'First to *what*?' Gus asked, mystified.

'See me,' Stevie said simply. 'You saw me, Gus. You were the first. Even before Alice did.'

Gus's head was spinning. Was he saying—?

'I've been waiting here a long time,' he added. 'Ever since my family left. I just can't believe she didn't come back for me.'

He stopped, as though pained. As though he might cry, Gus thought. Suddenly she recalled the article from Henry's manual for the Starlight. The one with the mother looking for her son, who she'd had to leave temporarily by the road. Could that have been about *Stevie*? But wouldn't that mean—?

'I remember when we arrived my mum saw Riley's Comet. The first time it was sighted in the southern hemisphere,' Stevie said.

She recalled what Ms McKenzie had said about the comet being a septuagenarian. The picture — a very sad picture — was starting to come into focus. 'You mean your family was here *seventy years ago*?' Gus replied. She remembered the story he had told her by the river, about the stone from space and his mother and then the bit about his family.

She did the maths quickly in her head. That would have been sometime in the 1950s. That would mean the boy would be old by now, a senior citizen like Henry. Unless that boy had ... died young ... and had stayed an eternal thirteen, haunting the Starlight ever since.

Her mind whirred like an insect's wings. Nicole had said this place was haunted and the townspeople had believed it — maybe they had been right. Maybe it had been *she*, Gus, who had got her ghosts mixed up.

'When they left me, I felt so lost. Even though the sign outside town told me I was in Calvary,' said Stevie, smiling sadly.

'What did you do?' Gus breathed.

'I camped by the river. For a few weeks I guess I just ... drifted. Then the Cronks opened the drive-in and I had the movies. I could sneak up and watch what was screening at the Starlight. I would pretend I was with this family, or that one. I liked to watch them, their faces so happy in the dark and then the burn of the screen.'

He paused.

'And I tried to fend for myself, but sometimes I got scared ...'

'So, what did you do? When you were afraid?'

'I hid in the cane, Gus.'

She looked at the bare burned paddock beyond the drive-in.

'I'm not from here,' Stevie explained. 'I didn't know about the harvest. The way they burn the cane.'

He stopped. Gus felt dread prickle up her spine.

'When the fire came, it was too late,' Stevie said. 'I ... I was in the canefield, hiding. I was too far in. And I couldn't escape, Gus, so I ... I ...'

'You died,' Gus whispered.

She thought she might stop breathing too, from sadness. She remembered the tall lanky figure she had seen coming out of the cane on the night of the first fire. It hadn't been Troy at all.

Stevie broke their silence. 'I guess I did, Gus, though I don't like to admit it. Even now. But I guess that's what happened to me.'

He swallowed. 'It hasn't been an easy time for me, Gus. There're a lot of angry ghosts about. Restless souls and you want to avoid them if you can. It's a dark place sometimes, this here in-between.'

She nodded, tears in her eyes.

'But then I met you and Alice,' Stevie continued. 'And I felt what I hadn't felt for a long time. I felt like I was part of something. Maybe even part of a family.'

Gus nodded. She felt like she was part of a family now too, though she supposed she always had been. It was Stevie who was alone. Then she recalled the last part of the article she had read in Henry's manual. Hadn't the article said the woman had come back for her son? It might have been too late, but she had come back all the same. Stevie deserved to know that. Maybe that's what he had been waiting for all this time. Ghosts always had some business they needed to resolve. 'Stevie, your mum came back for you,' she said.

He frowned. 'Thanks, Gus, but you don't know that.'

'Actually, I do,' Gus said. 'She really did. I read about it, in Henry's manual, which is like a whole collection of articles and photos and stuff about the Starlight and also Calvary. There was an article where your mum came here and asked the locals for help finding you.'

She was babbling. Stevie grimaced again.

Gus tried to recall some detail that would help Stevie believe her. She remembered there had been a quote about his sister. What had it said?

'Just a sec,' she said. 'Wait here. I'll be right back.'

She dashed to the caravan and retrieved Henry's manual from under the bed she shared with her brother and sister. She returned, puffing in the cool night air. She was gone only a minute or two, but Stevie seemed an even thinner version of himself.

'Thank you, Gus, but you really don't have to—'

'Was your sister's name Grace?' she interrupted.

Stevie's face went still. 'How ... how did you know that?' he asked, his voice faltering.

'It was in this article.' She thumbed frantically through the pages to show him. 'Look. See? Your mum said you were a good brother to your little sister, Gracie. She said they both missed you desperately.'

Stevie's face crumpled when he read the words. Gus wanted to put her arms around him, but he was of course a ghost.

'They came back for me,' he whispered.

'Yes,' said Gus. 'They really did.'

She was maybe even more glad than Stevie that they had.

'Thank you again, Gus. Really thank you. I guess I can … go now?' Stevie said, sounding as though he was seeing this truth as he spoke it.

'Wait, what?' Gus replied finding her voice again. 'Go where?'

'Where I've always been heading, I suppose. Someplace nice,' Stevie said. 'Someplace where my mum waits. Someplace like home.'

'But you've just come back. I feel like we've just got to know you,' she protested.

'Maybe I'll see you there, Gus,' Stevie said, as though he hadn't heard her. 'But not for a long time, I hope.'

And he started to vanish slightly, like mist in the morning.

'Wait, Stevie,' Gus said, panicked. Henry's manual slipped to the ground.

Stevie did not reply.

'Alice,' Gus called into the inky evening, alarmed.

'What is it, Gus?' Alice called.

Her sister appeared from a pocket of the night, much like a ghost herself. But when Alice put her hand on Gus's arm, she was warm and real.

Gus pointed at the disappearing form of Stevie, unable to find words for what she was seeing. His smile was still there, incandescent, while the rest of him was fading from sight.

'It's all right, Gus,' Alice said. 'It's OK.'

'But ...' Gus said, tears threatening to spill over her eyelashes.

'I know,' Alice said softly. 'But it's OK, Gus. We have to let him go.'

At a loss for words, feeling like she might melt too from sadness, Gus could only watch as Stevie disappeared from view. Her tears fell silently on the Starlight driveway.

Together the sisters stood, side by side in the dark

in the drive-in consumed by fire that was now their home.

Gus wiped her eyes with her sleeve and took a breath, the deepest breath she had ever breathed. Even though Stevie was gone, she had the sense that everything — finally — was going to be all right.

She turned to her sister, whose eyes were liquid comets in the dark. Alice too wiped her face with her sleeve. We are so alike, Gus realised. So much the same.

'So I *do* have it too,' Gus said.

Inside she was pinging. Though she would miss Stevie horribly, seeing him confirmed something, she had inherited the Able gift after all. The thought made her feel dizzy and scared and happy, all at once.

Gus took her sister's hand, supporting Alice as they walked back to the caravan. Tears ran down their faces and they both understood.

In the morning, Gus thought, she would take Alice to the river and show her sister the fragment of debris from outer space Stevie had hidden there. She knew where to find it. She would show Alice the crystalline veins of purple, blue and gold running through what looked like an otherwise ordinary rock.

Chapter 35

A week later, on Saturday morning, the Ables sat together around the table by the caravan in the winter sun. They were joined by the real-life Henry Cronk.

This time, they sat at a camping table Henry had lent them, along with some outdoor chairs he had rustled up. All their things were packed up in the suitcases by the caravan door. They had been expecting Henry to come today.

Watching him tuck into the pikelets Mrs Able had made for morning tea, in the caravan's tiny kitchenette, Gus found it hard to believe she had ever thought him a ghost. Henry spread another pikelet with jam and handed it to Artie, who crammed the whole thing in his mouth in one go.

Alice also buttered a pikelet, a double one made

of two that had merged together while cooking in the pan, and handed half to Gus. They all chewed in silence.

Mrs Able appeared from inside the caravan carrying a pot of tea. She joined them at the table and poured Henry and herself a cuppa.

'Thank you for letting us stay on a few more days,' Mrs Able said, handing him an orange mug. 'It's allowed me to sort some things out.'

'How did you go with the police business?' Henry enquired.

'Terry's going to help organise the car transport from my mother's place. And the stealing charges will be dropped, thank goodness. I can prove Troy was trying to extort my, ah, abilities. And also that we really needed to get away from that house.'

'That's wonderful news, Delphine,' Henry said. 'I'm sure that it was extremely stressful living under those conditions. I'm no stranger to extortion myself.'

They all paused to consider the spot where the Starlight screen had stood.

'Anyway, it's been very kind of you,' said Mrs Able, after a while. 'It's nice the kids got to say goodbye to their friends at school.'

Gus had nearly been in tears when she had said goodbye to Nicole. It was wonderful and tough, as well as strange and sad and satisfying, to have a friend. The girls had promised to email each other once Gus's family settled somewhere new. So far the plan was to drive to Gran's and put Troy's car on a transport truck from there. They would attend the local school while their mum looked for work. They'd stay with Gran just until they got on their feet, their mother said.

'It is nice,' Henry agreed. 'In fact, that's what I wanted to talk to you about this morning. Friends, and staying on a little longer, I mean.'

'I — I don't understand,' said Mrs Able.

'I'll just come out with it then. I've been thinking I'd like to rebuild the Starlight.'

'*Rebuild*? That does sound wonderful. But how?'

They all regarded the empty site, where dirt mingled with ash.

'Well, there's only one way I know of and that's to pay someone,' Henry replied.

'But after the fire was found to be lit deliberately … I mean, it's not really my business, but won't you have trouble getting the insurance money?'

'It's possible, yes,' Henry conceded. 'But I'm told

by the authorities it's clear I had nothing to do with Deirdre's actions. And luckily I have assets, beyond possessing all my own hair, I mean.' He paused and they all looked at him open-mouthed. 'I'm planning to sell my house in town.'

'Your house?' Mrs Able repeated. 'You can't do that, Mr Cronk. Where will you live?'

All three children looked at the caravan.

'Oh,' said their mother. 'Of course.'

'Oh no,' said Henry, quickly. 'I'll stay in my river hut.'

'Your *river hut*?' Mrs Able echoed. 'Is that safe?'

'It's perfectly fine and very suited to my needs. I built it myself, years ago. Besides, I like living by the river. The breeze and the sound of the water and the bird life. I like it better than living in town.'

'It is pretty cool down there,' Gus interjected.

'Still, it's your home,' said their mother. 'You must have made so many memories there ... and to rebuild the Starlight will take time. Are you sure?'

'Since I plan on being around for some time yet —' here he cast a look at Gus, who blushed '— I want to rebuild this place. The Starlight means everything to me. It's been my life.'

'Yes,' said their mother, 'I can understand that. This place had, *has*, a special quality about it. It's magical, almost. We've loved our time here, brief as it's been.'

'I noticed that,' Henry agreed. 'When you're retired like me, you have a decent amount of time to think. It's not often you see someone with such business nous. And you've got an asset in these children here, too. Since you've all been doing such a good job, Mrs Able, I was wondering if, when the time comes to open the Starlight again, you would be interested in managing it?'

Mrs Able was speechless. The children looked at each other in amazement. Gus answered for her. She didn't want Henry to retract the offer. 'She'd love to. Even if we are *amateurs*.'

'Gus,' admonished their mother.

'I suppose I had that coming,' said Henry.

'It would be an honour,' said Mrs Able, finding her voice again. 'But when … when might that be?'

'I intend to start as soon as possible. We'll rebuild the Moonbeam first. If we get the cafe up and running, you can serve meals while we wait for the Starlight to be constructed. Stagger the build, and the income streams. Would you be interested in that?'

'She is definitely interested in that,' said Gus. 'Our mum's an excellent cook.'

Her brother and sister looked at her, aghast. But in that moment, they realised it was actually true. They all laughed in shock.

'Good,' Henry said, when they finally stopped. 'We'll budget for a modest manager's residence on site. How does that sound?'

'A manager's *house*?' Gus's mother breathed. 'I reckon we can wait for that.'

'Until then, you'll have to stay in the caravan, I'm afraid, if you can hack it,' said Henry.

'It's grown on me, actually,' admitted their mother.

Gus agreed. Being so close to her family had grown on her too.

'I'm pleased to hear it,' Henry said. 'We'll also still need a Head of Box Office and General Manager, as well as a Head Projectionist, of course. By the time it's built, Gus should be the legal working age. Alice already is, of course. No more child labour.'

He smiled at the girls.

'I don't mind helping out,' said Alice.

'Me either,' Gus chimed in.

'You can pay me in Transformers,' Artie suggested.

'It's a deal,' said Henry. 'The only question is, how are you going to get by until it's built and we're operational?'

'I do have another skillset I could use in the meantime to pay the bills,' Mrs Able said, with slight hesitation.

'I had heard about your psychic abilities,' Henry said nodding. 'I imagine it can be draining on a person.'

Mrs Able nodded. 'Sometimes,' she agreed. 'But this time I'd be my own manager. I'd be doing it on my own terms. And not from home.'

'You could be a mobile medium,' Gus suggested. 'And I'm sure my friend Nicole's mum would be able to help you get a stall at the local markets. She sells dream catchers,' she informed Henry.

Mrs Able smiled.

'You know, thanks to Gus's comet screening and the full house, I've been able to start saving to buy a car.'

'It's all coming together nicely,' said Henry, sounding pleased.

'Almost,' said Mrs Able. She paused. 'Henry, I have to ask you something. In my capacity as the new manager.'

'Fire away,' said Henry.

She took a deep breath, 'What do you think about the Starlight going digital?'

'Do you mean all that new internet fandangle?' Henry demanded. 'That wi-fi rot?'

He pronounced it 'whiffy'.

'Yes,' said Mrs Able. 'Exactly. I realise it's expensive, but I've been reading about the quality of the technology now and the audience experience. You'd need to install a server and these days the movies come on a hard drive. I think we could cover the costs of a digital upgrade of the Starlight if we expand our marketing strategy. If we were to consider, say, attracting tourist traffic as well as the local market, given we're located so close to the highway.'

'That sounds reasonable and you do use impressive words, Delphine. I suppose I don't have a choice, do I?' Henry replied ruefully.

'No,' agreed Mrs Able and they laughed.

'I'm lucky I've got you lot to drag me into the twenty-first century,' Henry said, affectionately. 'If only Deirdre had wanted to work *with* me, instead of have me sign the place over to her.' Henry contemplated the space where the screen had stood. 'I've always just wanted the best for this place. For everybody's sake,' he said. He looked down the hill towards town. They all followed his gaze. 'Well, I'd best be off. If we're going to do this, I'd better get cracking on cleaning up my house for sale.'

'We'll help you,' said Mrs Able decisively. 'We've gotten pretty good at cleaning lately! Write down your address for me and we'll come by this afternoon, after I've told Terry the new plan and arranged to send back Troy's car from here. You don't have a choice on this one either, Henry.'

'Managers,' grumbled Henry. But he was smiling.

'Take some pikelets for the road,' their mother added. 'And Henry? Thank you.' Her eyes were shining as she handed him a plate of morning tea.

'No need to make a fuss,' said Henry gruffly. But he accepted the food and Gus noticed him smile as he turned to head back to his car.

'Oh, I almost forgot,' said Henry, reaching into his fishing jacket. 'I found this outside, over there. I believe you were the last to have it, Gus.'

He handed her a battered leather-bound book. It was Henry's manual for the Starlight.

'Thank you,' Gus said, confused. 'I'm sorry, I dropped it when ... when—'

'It's alright,' Henry said gently, 'I know you'll take good care of it from now on.'

'Thank you,' Gus said again. 'I will. But shouldn't you be giving this to Mum?'

'Well, she is the Business Manager,' Henry agreed. 'But this is an operating manual for the Head Projectionist.'

Like the first time she had seen the projector, she felt spangly inside. She opened the manual. On the first page was the list of names of the Starlight operators. There was Henry's name and his dates working as the projectionist and before that, Henry's father's name, George Cronk, with the dates from when he had opened the place and when he handed it over to his son.

The last name on the list was hers: Gus Able, projectionist from today's date and a dash.

'Thank you, Henry,' she said.

She was glad he had forgiven her for thinking he was dead. She tried not to let him see the tear slipping down her nose.

Her name was there, in the history of the Starlight. And there was no end date, which meant they were staying for as long as they liked. The book had a lot of blank pages left too.

They had a place of their own now, Gus realised, even if it was a haunted drive-in, where they lived in a caravan smelling of possum wee. But they were all invited to be part of something new coming to this town. She could feel happiness vibrating off everyone around the table. Wait until I tell Nicole we're staying, she thought. She couldn't wait for school on Monday.

As she watched Henry get into his car, Gus thought she might just try her luck and get a permanent library card when they next went into town.